THE OTHER SIDE
OF THE CLYDE

THE OTHER SIDE OF THE CLYDE

Edited by David Drever
& Liam Stewart

Hodder & Stoughton

A MEMBER OF THE HODDER HEADLINE GROUP

British Library Cataloguing in Publication Data

Other Side of the Clyde. – New ed
 I. Drever, David II. Stewart, Liam
 820.809411

ISBN 0–340–61132–4

This edition first published 1994
Impression number   10 9 8 7 6 5 4 3 2 1
Year   1999 1998 1997 1996 1995 1994

Typeset by Wearset, Boldon, Tyne and Wear.
Printed in Great Britain for Hodder & Stoughton Educational, a division of Hodder Headline Plc, 338 Euston Road, London NW1 3BH by St. Edmundsbury Press, Bury St. Edmunds, Suffolk.

Acknowledgements

The editors and publishers would like to thank the following for granting their permission to reproduce copyright material in this book:

'Blood' by Keith Aitchison, 'Staff of Life' by Arthur Young and 'The Ferry' by Alan Spence from *Scottish Short Stories*, published by Harper Collins Ltd; 'Barely An Incident' from *Red Tides* by Dilys Rose, published by Martin Secker & Warburg; 'Vymura: The Shade Card Poem' and 'Fat Girl's Confession' by Liz Lochhead, published by Polygon Books; 'Saturday Song' by Maureen Monaghan reproduced by kind permission of the author; 'Almost Miss Scotland' from *Bagpipe Muzak* by Liz Lochhead, published by Penguin Books, 1991, copyright © Liz Lochhead, 1991; 'Four of the Belt', 'Moral Philosophy' and 'Mr Endrews Speaks' by Tom Leonard from *Intimate Voices*, published by Galloping Dog Press; 'Chapter 6: The Telling Part', 'Chapter 7: Black Bottom' and 'My Grandmother's Houses' from *The Adoption Papers* by Jackie Kay, published by Bloodaxe Books, 1991; 'Eugenesis' and 'Initiation' by William McIlvanney from *In Through the Head*, published by Mainstream Publishing Co (Edinburgh) Ltd; 'Not the Burrell Collection' by Edwin Morgan, published by Moriscat Press; 'The Glasgow Subway Poems' from *Collected Poems* by Edwin Morgan, published by Carcanet Press Ltd; 'After the War' from *The Happier Life* by Douglas Dunn and 'Washing the Coins' from *St Kilda's Parliament* by Douglas Dunn, both published by Faber and Faber Ltd; 'Oor Hamlet' and 'The Scottish Song' by Adam McNaughton reproduced by kind permission of the author; 'The Great McGunnigle' by Edward Boyle reproduced by kind permission of the author; 'First Foot' by Janice Galloway reproduced by kind permission of the author; 'Sharon, the Ferryman's Daughter' by Valerie Thornton reproduced by kind permission of the author; 'The New Boy' by Geddes Thompson reproduced by kind permission of the author; 'The Star' by Alasdair Gray reproduced by kind permission of the author.

Every effort has been made to trace and acknowledge ownership of copyright. The publishers will be glad to make suitable arrangements with any copyright holders whom it has not been possible to contact.

Contents

Contents

Introduction

Two boys cross the Clyde, hoping to find a new world of
adventure and excitement; a Glasgow youth is drawn to
Belfast after a visit from his uncle, an IRA hero; a
shocking childhood experience puts a boy off rhubarb for
the rest of his life; a posh girl from the suburbs enters the
life of an unemployed boy from a housing estate; school
term opens with the prospect of having to face the dreaded
McGunnigle once again; Oor Hamlet kills his stepfather;
Miss Scotland walks out; a victim of racial harassment
fights back . . .

These stories and poems are mainly about the people of
Glasgow and its nearby towns and countryside. A few take
place in the past, dealing with a way of life that is now
gone. Most of them feature topics that concern us now.
Like all cities, Glasgow is best observed when its people
talk. The people in the following pages speak in their
everyday language – they use words that are sometimes
strange but also very real. These poems and stories are
about ordinary people at extraordinary times in their lives.
We hope they say something to you and, above all, we
hope you find them good reading.

David Drever and Liam Stewart, 1994

SECTION I

Stories

THE FERRY
Alan Spence

The cane arrow rose in the still warm air. Aleck and Joe shielded their eyes from the sun and watched its flight. It seemed to rise clear of the tenements that enclosed them and hang for a moment against the sky before turning back to complete its arc and fall to land with a jar that staved and shuddered its whole length on the hardpacked dirt and brick of the back court.

'It's a goodyin!' said Joe, grinning and flexing the bow that Aleck had just made. The bow had fired its first shot, and it was good. Aleck nodded and set about making a bow for himself as Joe ran across to pick up the arrow.

They had bought six bits of bamboo cane. Each was long enough to make a bow or be broken in half to make two arrows.

Aleck was stringing the bows, notching each end for the string to fit, and Joe was making the arrows. If he had simply snapped the canes in half the pieces would have split, leaving each arrow a loose mess of fibres and split ends. So he used an old hacksaw blade to cut carefully through each cane before breaking it and binding each end with black insulating tape.

They played at their craft with seriousness. They were crouched in a clearing. The grey buildings were their jungle and the fragments of stone and broken glass they had gathered and laid out were imagined arrowheads of flint and bone.

The hacksaw blade cutting through the cane sometimes made a harsh rasping noise that set Aleck's teeth on edge. Like the squeak of polystyrene rubbed on a window. Like the scrape and squeal of the teacher's chalk on the blackboard.

(Guide-lines for her chalk against the black – like the lines on the pages of his jotter – date in the lefthand margin – NAME in the middle of the top line – below that (miss two lines) the title of the composition – 'What I want to be' – sun shafting in through the window, lighting on dancing particles of dust – dust of chalk in the air – sunlight – what I want – to be.)

At the beginning of the long summer holidays it had seemed as if they could never end. Eight weeks was an eternity stretching before them. Now, incredibly, five of those precious weeks had passed.

'Imagine huvin tae go back tae school 'n a cuppla weeks,' said Aleck.

'You're no sa bad,' said Joe. 'Youse Proddies uv goat a week merr than us.'

'Ach well,' said Aleck. 'Youse ur always gettin hoalidays a obligation. Jist wan saint efter another. Ah think we should get an extra two weeks tae make up fur it.'

Joe stuck out his tongue and gave Aleck the V-sign. Then he grinned.

'Heh Aleck, comin wull no bother gawn back tae school? Wull jist run away an dog it forever.'

'That wid be brilliant!' said Aleck. 'Wherr could we go?'

Joe held up his arrow.

'We could go tae America an live wi REAL Indians. Ah've goat an auntie in Canada.'

'Ach thur's nae real Indians left,' said Aleck. 'They aw get pit oot 'n daft wee reservations.'

'How aboot India then?' said Joe. 'Or Africa? We could live in a tree hoose.'

'Pick bananas 'n oranges,' said Aleck.

'Hunt animals.'

'Make pals wi some a them but,' said Aleck. 'Lions 'n tigers an that.'

'Great white chiefs. Me chief Joseph.' He pouted his lips and spoke in as deep a voice as he could, beating his chest with his fist.

'Me chief Alexander,' said Aleck, raising his bow. 'We wid huv tae gie wursels better names but.'

'Walla Walla Wooski!' said Joe.

'We could paint wursels tae,' said Aleck. 'Werr feathers an bones.'

'Imagine bein cannibals,' said Joe. 'We could jist eat white men that got loast in the jungle.'

'Fancy gawn intae the chippy,' said Aleck, 'an askin fur two single fish an a whiteman supper!'

(Louie in the chip shop – like Sweeney Todd – cutting people up for pies – rubbing his hands and gloating over the carcass of a fat schoolboy – ambushed in the back court.)

'People ur supposed tae taste like pork,' Aleck said at last. 'Think ah'll stoap eatin meat.'

'Ach don't be daft,' said Joe. 'If we didnae eat animals we'd get ett wursels.'

'Suppose so,' said Aleck.

He put the finishing touches to his bow. Joe taped the last arrowhead. They went padding off across Congos and Zambezis of their own making, to see what was to be hunted.

Aleck lay with his eyes closed on the flat roof of the midden, the warmth of the sun on his bare arms and legs, his face against the stone. And nothing existed outside himself in that moment. (Colour, mainly red, behind his eyes – warm, warm – low sounds, a feeling, a murmur – flies, drone – voices far away – a dream, faint breeze – laughter, a car, tin can dropped in a bin – warm, he lay like some great slow lizard, coiled and lazing on a warm rock – he could almost remember it.)

He sat up suddenly and looked around. The colours were still behind his eyes. He focused on Joe on the ground below, stalking a pigeon. Joe. The back court. Hunting. It was real. He was Aleck. His whole life had actually happened.

Joe shot his arrow and the pigeon flustered off to circle round and perch on a railing.

3

'Bastard!' said Joe.

The arrow skimmed the wall where the pigeon had sat and landed on the other side in the next back court.

'Gonnae nik doon an get that Aleck?' said Joe, looking up.

From his high perch on the dyke Aleck could see both back courts.

'Ther's some fullas watchin yer doo,' he said. 'Thu'll prob'ly huv the perry us fur tryin tae shoot it.'

Aleck climbed down on to the wall.

'If ye hear me gettin mangled yull know whit's happened,' he said.

'Ach well,' said Joe, 'it wis nice knowin ye.'

Aleck dropped down on to the other side of the wall.

The men gave no sign that they had even noticed him but he hesitated to move for the arrow, which had landed almost at their feet.

It was funny to think of them as bird-watchers. Most of them were in their twenties or thirties, one or two were older. Men without jobs who seemed to spend their whole time loafing or shambling around, always in a cluster, scuffling and shabby, always finding ways to fill the time till the glorious weekend when there was money for wine and they were loud and alive and glowing, singing and fighting and sick.

Watching the pigeons was a mystery with its secrets, its initiates, a language of its own. They would cup their hands to their mouths and echo the bird's own call. They used strange words like fantail and others that Aleck could never quite make out or understand. Some of them even built wooden doocots, box-hutches where the birds could feed. Doocot meant dovecot because doo was short for dove. Dovecot. Cot for a dove. But the pigeons were mostly grey, although if you could look closely you might see colours. Like an oil stain on the road under the light. Gurgling and strutting and grey. Doves should be soft and graceful and white. Like the dove sent from the ark, to find land where it could rest. Miss Riddie had told them the story and taught them the song.

(The words chalked on the blackboard – teacher with her pointer – repeat after me –

O that I had wings like a dove
Then I would fly away and be at rest
Lo then would I wander far off
And remain in the wilderness

di dum diddy dum diddy dum / diddy dum diddy dum didum.)
One of the men picked up the arrow. He looked straight at
Aleck and snapped the arrow in two. He was grinning.
'Aw . . . izzat no a shame . . . ah've went an broke it!'
The others laughed and he threw the pieces aside.
'Get tae buggery wi yer bows 'n arras or ah'll snap yer bloody
neck!'
Aleck ran and scrambled back across the wall.
The pigeon rose and soared over the rooftops and out of
sight.

The afternoon sticky and hot and the pavement tar soft and
melting. Aleck and Joe were scraping their initials with their
arrows.
(The way the tar opened under the pressure – glistening black
scar on the pavement's dusty grey – initials – names.)
'Tar's brilliant stuff, intit,' said Joe.
'So it is,' said Aleck. 'See the smell aff it when it's jist been laid!
Makes ye wanty sink yer teeth inty it!'
'So it dis. Ah love smells lik that.'
'The smell a the subway!'
'New shoe boaxes!'
'Rubber tyres!'
'Terrific!'
Joe dug into the tar, wound the arrow till its end was coiled
and clogged.
'Looks like a big toly disn't it!'
They dug out lumps with their hands, kneaded and stretched
and smeared it.
'Really dis make ye wanty eat it.'
'D'you remember eatin sand when ye wur wee?' asked Aleck.
'Naw, ah don't think so,' said Joe. 'How, d'you?'
'Aye. Sandpies it wis. Looked great. Tasted horrible but.'

(Mouthful of dirt – becoming mud – grit between the teeth.)

'Jesus!' said Joe. 'How ur we gonnae get this stuff aff?'

Aleck looked at his blackened hands. 'Margarine's supposed tae take it aff,' he said.

'We could always leave them,' said Joe. 'Cover wursels in it.'

'Fur gawn tae the jungle,' said Aleck. He picked up his bow and arrows.

'Ach look at that!' said Joe. His arrow had split digging into the tar. He threw it away, disgusted.

'Never mind,' said Aleck. ''Mon wull go up tae mah hoose'n clean it aff.'

Margarine smeared on their tarry hands, a greasy mess, the fat and the tar merging to make a mucky green as they rubbed and scraped and tried to clean it off.

'Horrible, intit?' said Joe, looking at his hands.

'Imagine seein thaym comin ower yer shooder'n a dark night,' said Aleck. He wailed and thrust gnarled slimy claws towards Joe. They stalked each other round the kitchen, menacing the furniture with green and trembling werewolf paws.

'Smelly,' said Aleck, stopping in mid-growl to sniff his hands. He went to the sink and tried washing them clean under the tap but the cold water couldn't dissolve the grease which still clung in globules and streaks.

'Ah canny really be bothered bilin up a kettle a watter,' he said.

'Gie's up that auld towel aff the flerr, wull ye?'

With the towel they managed to rub off most of the dirt.

'At's no bad,' said Joe. 'Prob'ly werr aff in a day ur two.'

They looked at the dirt still ingrained in the skin and under their nails.

'Dead quiet,' said Joe, unaccustomed to the emptiness of the house. Joe had brothers and sisters and his house was always loud with their noise.

'Suppose so,' said Aleck.

The tick of the clock. Stillness. Noises from the back court.

'Think ah'll jist stey in,' said Aleck. 'That's hauf four the noo, an ma mammy'll be hame fae ur work at five.'

'When dis yer da get in?' asked Joe.

'Aboot hauf five ur somethin.'

Joe lifted his bow and moved towards the door.

'Fancy gin doon tae the ferry efter tea?' he said.

'The ferry?'

'Aye, we could nik acroass tae Partick an play aboot therr 'nen come back. Disnae cost anythin.'

'At's a great idea,' said Aleck. 'See ye efter tea then.'

He handed Joe one of his arrows.

'Here,' he said. 'That's us git wan each.'

Past a pub with a cluster of neon grapes above the door, past a mission hall called Bethel, left off Govan Road and along a narrow lane, through the docks to the ferry steps.

Ferry steps. They were often invoked as part of a prophecy, against the drunk and incapable. Spat out like a curse – 'That yin'll finish up at the fit a the ferry steps.'

Aleck and Joe sat at the top of the steep slippery wooden steps, waiting for the ferry to cross from the Partick side.

'Imagine slippin fae here,' said Joe. 'Ye'd jist tummel right in.'

They looked in silence, down to where the steps disappeared into black invisible depth, the oily river lapping softly.

'Here it comes!' said Aleck.

They stood up and watched as the squat brown ferry chugged across towards them.

The water swirled up the steps as it bumped and thudded to rest.

The ferry had the same kind of low dumpy bulk as a tug, though it was much smaller. It had a long low deck with sides to a height of about three feet running along its whole length and open at each end. Spanning the middle section was a canopy. This gave shelter for the passengers in the rain and also covered the pilot's wheel-house. The whole ferry, including the canopy, was painted the same dull brown.

Aleck and Joe went to the front and leaned over the side. Smoke phutted from the chimney as the ferry chugged its way out. Joe had left his bow at home but Aleck had brought his with him, the one remaining arrow tucked under his belt. He trailed the bow in the water, watching the wake ripple out behind it, the boat rocking gently beneath them, the feel of the deck through their thin-soled shoes.

Towering along both banks were the great jutting cranes of the shipyards, a tanker further downstream, gulls circling overhead.

They'd been told a little about the river in school. How it began as a trickle away in the southern uplands and wound its way down through sheep farms and mining towns and eventually flowed through Glasgow and beyond to the firth and the open sea.

'Funny tae think'n aw this watter comin fae a wee stream up'n the hills,' said Aleck.

'Intit,' said Joe.

'Ah mean, the same watter,' said Aleck.

They were silent, looking down at the oily flow. Grey with colours. Like the pigeon.

The journey was too quickly over. At the Partick side they charged up the steps then stopped and looked around them. The ferry started back across.

Miss Riddie had told them about Partick and Govan growing side by side. The deepening of the river. Shipbuilding. Cheap houses for the shipyard workers. She had said they were like reflections, Partick and Govan, with the river like a mirror in between.

The grey buildings looked the same, but they were not their own. They felt lost and threatened. The strange streets and unfamiliar faces were hostile. At the corner opposite, a group of men loafing. Boys their own age, playing, looking towards them. They would have to go past them to get clear of the ferry.

'D'you know anywherr tae go?' asked Aleck.

'Naw. No really,' said Joe.

'D'ye fancy jist gawn back?'

'Comin?'

'Right, c'mon!'

They squatted on the steps waiting. If Partick and Govan were on opposite sides of the mirror, only one side was real. It depended on where you had been brought up. And for Aleck and

Joe, Govan was the only reality they knew. When they were back
once more on the steps at the Govan side, Joe turned to Aleck.

'Heh! D'ye fancy jist steyin oan the ferry an gawn back an
furrat a coupla times? Jist fur a wee hurl?'

'At's a great idea!' said Aleck. They jumped back on to the ferry
just in time before it moved off.

The low sun was bright on the water and the shadows it cast
were long. 'Heh Aleck,' said Joe. 'Ye could haud up the driver wi
yer bow'n arra an get um tae take us tae America or Africa or
wherrever it wis.'

'Imagine!' said Aleck. He looked at the bow. 'Och wid ye lookit
the state ae it!' The string had split the cane at one end and the
split had continued half-way down its length.

'Never mind,' said Joe.

'Disnae really matter, ah suppose.'

At the Partick side they decided to jump off and join the
oncoming passengers for the journey back, just for the sake of the
leap from the deck to the steps. But when they tried to get back on
the pilot blocked their way.

'Right!' he said. 'Yizzur steyin aff. Yizzuv bin up an doon aff
this boat lik a bloody yoyo. D'ye think it's jist fur playin oan? Noo
goan! Get!'

They stood helpless, watching as the ferry moved off towards
their home shore.

'Whit'll we dae noo?' asked Aleck.

'There's another ferry up at the Art Galleries,' said Joe. 'We
could walk it up.'

'Wull that no take us a while?' said Aleck.

'Nothin else we kin dae.' Joe looked out after the ferry, now
almost at the Govan side.

'Bastard!' he said.

Aleck threw his split bow and his last arrow into the water and
watched them being swirled out by the current. He wondered
how far they would be carried. Out past the shipyards, past
Greenock and Gourock to the firth, past the islands, out past
Ireland, out to the Atlantic, out . . .

Aleck suddenly shivered. The sky was beginning to darken.

The river was deep and wide. They were far from home, in an alien land.

'Bloody Partick,' said Joe.

They began the slow climb to the top of the ferry steps.

BLOOD
Keith Aitchison

It was a sunny week in late August, when the heat curled along the streets and up the tenement stairs of the baker's oven of a city, that Timothy Maguire came to stay with his widowed sister and his nephew.

'By God, have I not brought the good weather with me!' he exclaimed, putting down his suitcase and beaming at them, his round face shining with sweat.

'Mary!' he embraced his sister, then thrust out his hand. 'And this hulking giant cannot be young Martin?'

'I'm nineteen, Uncle Tim.' Martin's hand was gripped.

'Nineteen, is it?' Timothy whistled. 'By God, there's time passed, and a lot of Maguire grown in this lad, Mary. Does he not look like our father when young?'

'He has the eyes, just. The face is his own father's. Come, sit down.'

Timothy sat and pulled out a handkerchief to mop his face and the wet, darkened roots of his fair hair. 'And how is it with you both?' he asked.

'Martin grows up, and I grow older,' said Mary, and plucked at a lock of her hair. 'Do you see the grey?'

'No more than before.'

'That was four years ago. The funeral.'

'Ah, I meant to come sooner. But business, and other things. You should have come to me for a time.'

'I don't think Belfast is the place for holidays now.'

'Maybe not. It's remarkable how you get accustomed to it all, though.' Timothy paused. 'And it's not as if the cause were not just.'

'The cause!' Mary shook her head. 'You're the son of your father, right enough.'

'And proud of it,' Timothy smiled. 'Was he not a great man after all?'

'What cause?' Martin interjected, curious.

11

'You don't know?' Timothy stared in amazement, round eyes in a round face.

'That's enough.' Mary rose sharply, and Timothy thought that right enough the years and the widowing had taken more from her than she deserved to lose.

'What cause?' asked Martin once more. 'Ireland?'

'Ireland! Of course, Ireland,' said Timothy with relief. 'Thank God you've not lost your heritage entirely.'

'Half his heritage, or more likely, remembering mother's opinions, one quarter,' said Mary, going into the scullery and speaking back over her shoulder. 'And remember his father, and his side of the family.'

'Aren't they Irish too, with the name O'Brien?' asked Timothy.

'No one remembers when they came over, but it was long ago. And it's near tea-time.'

'The blood's the same. The years don't change it.'

'Ah, the old blood, who knows who else has got into it over the centuries,' said Mary sourly, 'and bugger the old blood for any argument.'

Martin's jaw dropped at the flaring of his mother's temper. Timothy winked at him and gave a long whistle.

'The language!' he called. 'That's my mother's daughter right enough.'

'Who else would put up with you?' Mary asked back, but her voice was no longer sour.

'Do you remember the time mother lost her temper with that butcher in Foyle Street, the one who sold her the wormy meat?'

They laughed together, good humour restored, and Timothy went to his suitcase and brought out a bottle of Irish whiskey.

'Just an aperitif, as the French say.' He poured three glasses. 'It's a great pity James is not still with us, he loved a good whiskey.'

'He never refused any whiskey, good or bad,' said Mary, with neither malice nor sadness, turning her head to smile at Martin and show she was not serious.

'Well now, Martin.' Timothy watched approvingly as his nephew swallowed the whiskey. 'I'll be looking to you to show me around Glasgow. I don't know it at all.'

'You'll have an advantage then,' said Mary. 'Most who do know it well have had to forget the half of what they know in order to find out where they are.'

'Redevelopment?'

'That's the name they give it, the smart name so that we won't notice the way they've ruined the city.'

'The progress is a great thing for them as makes money from it.'

Martin listened to them talk, hearing them drift back down the years to their shared memories. The talk, the memories and the unaccustomed whiskey had softened the Glasgow in his mother's voice. The more she spoke, the more an underlying Belfast edge cut through in the words, as if an echo from the past.

'Tell me, how's young Mary and her man?' asked Timothy suddenly. 'Do you hear from them at all?'

'I do. They're both well, down there in Leeds, and I'm to visit in October and see their new house.'

'New house?' Timothy whistled. 'They must be doing well. And you, young Martin, are you going to visit your sister?'

'No,' said Martin. 'I hope to have found work by then, or else I'll still be looking for it.'

After they had eaten, and after Timothy had remarked that Mary's cooking was still the best east of home, he followed Martin back down the winding stairs and out into the evening, with the tenement shadow sweeping down in a cooling tide along the length of the street, still pleasantly warm for a stroll in shirt-sleeves, with the children calling and playing around the close-mouths of the grey tenements curving towards the heart of the city.

Timothy and Martin strolled along the pavement to the main road, and watched the pedestrians and traffic, the city's people in sunlit evening hours between their day and sleep. The doors of the pubs were opened to any cooling breeze, and the sounds of talk and laughter, the clinking of glasses and bottles breathed out on to the pavements in a warm beery invitation.

'When I was in France,' said Timothy, 'the pubs would have

tables on the street, where you could sit on evenings like this and take a cool glass. It's a pity we couldn't do that tonight.'

'We haven't the weather for it,' said Martin apologetically. 'It's not like this very often.'

'Still, it would make a great sight, would it not? The Glasgow topers sitting in the rain outside every pub, with their glasses filling up with water and the waiters in mackintoshes and Wellington boots. People would pay to see that.'

Martin laughed, beginning to warm to his uncle's humour.

'And no soldiers,' Timothy mused, watching a group of young men pass by joking among themselves. 'You don't know how lucky you are, Martin. No soldiers, and nobody afraid.'

'I see it on the television,' said Martin, awkward with the sudden change.

'Your television is censored, I'll tell you that. They don't dare to show you even one half of what the soldiers do, over there.'

Martin shuffled his feet, uncomfortable with this grim note in Timothy.

'Ah well,' Timothy slapped Martin's back. 'Why talk of that now? Your lives aren't touched by it, thank God, and I'm on holiday.'

'And do you see,' he continued, 'how the pubs in this street are positively entreating us to cross their thresholds. Are you a drinking man, now?'

'I take a pint or two,' admitted Martin.

'And two it will be,' said Timothy, and steered his nephew into the nearest pub.

A pint in his fist, Timothy took a long pull and smacked his lips. He looked around the pub with a seasoned eye, noting the long formica bar with plain mirrors behind and the gantries on either side. There were little tables in the corners, and over it all a cloud of cigarette smoke and the hard language of men drinking with no women in the company.

'A man's pub,' Timothy observed. 'You wouldn't be bringing your girlfriends here, Martin?'

'I haven't got one, just now.'

'No? Playing the field, is it?'

'Playing nothing. I've no work, Uncle Tim,' Martin felt

ashamed, knowing there was no cause for shame. 'No money, no girlfriend.'

'Just "Tim", eh? I'm your mother's younger brother,' Timothy said, and sighed. 'So, no work and no girl. That's hard. And you'll need the job to get the money to find a girl.'

'I had work. But they laid us off, and it's been the dole for three months.'

'Ah, it's hard. I've been without work myself so I know. I do joinery now, my own boss and it keeps me going.'

Timothy looked around the bar, and the smile returned to his face.

'How do you spend your time?' he asked. 'Do you watch the football?'

'The Celtic.' Martin's chin lifted. 'I go to Parkhead with my mates in the season, when we've got the money. We can't afford the away matches.'

'And tell me, is there that powerful atmosphere we hear about? Songs and the Irish flag waving?'

'Songs and chants,' Martin flushed with the alcohol's gift of enthusiasm. 'When we play Rangers, we do it all specially to annoy the Orangemen. We sing the Soldiers' Song and chant "IRA – all the way!" and all that! It's great!'

'Is it now?' Timothy laughed and emptied his glass. 'Well, that sounds like the sons of Erin to me.'

He stood up to make his way to the bar, counting out money into his hand. Martin started to rise, reaching for the pound notes in his hip pocket.

'I'll get this one.'

'You will not,' Timothy reached out with a work-hardened hand and held him down in his seat. 'These are on me, and no arguments.'

It seemed to Martin as if for once a week passed too quickly. He spent his days and evenings with Timothy. Once, they took the train to Edinburgh, together with Mary, and on another day, a glaring hot day, the three of them went down to Largs and passed the day in sunshine on the sand and in the water. That evening, Timothy took them for dinner in a white-fronted restaurant with ropes looped ship-fashion around the balcony rails, and they ate and drank royally at a white-clothed table looking out at the sea and the hills of Arran.

It seemed to Martin that Timothy had lifted him from the grey drudgery of unemployment, and it was a feeling of gratitude, together with his natural liking for his uncle, that brought them as close and familiar as any friends.

A question of his grandfather began to build in Martin's mind. He had never known him, and somehow the subject had never arisen at home, or perhaps it had been deliberately avoided. As the week passed, with Timothy's presence the vacuum of his mother's Irish family began to fill in patches, like clouds gathering in a clear sky, and subtly altered the way in which Martin saw himself. He remembered Timothy speaking: 'A great man after all,' and curiosity nagged at him with the persistence of toothache, now sharp and demanding, now dull and weak, but always unavoidably claiming his attention, and refusing quiescence.

The night before Timothy left for home, the pair of them travelled to a famously Irish bar on the south side of the city. The evening began to a medley of soft Irish songs played and sung by a blackbrowed accordionist, and later, as the drink flowed both into him and into his audience, and the clouds of cigarette smoke streamed up through the evening to the yellow ceiling, the soft lilts of the Gael gradually made way for the harsher war songs and proud laments of the Fenian men and the IRA. Timothy sang with others in the bar, a mellow baritone in 'Sean South', and even 'The Belfast Brigade', and Martin listened and drank among the other descendants of expatriate Irish, and was swept along on their hazy tides of emotion.

'Tell me about grandfather,' he asked Timothy. 'You said I resemble him.'

Timothy leaned back in his chair and looked at Martin, raising and dropping his eyebrows, crinkling and smoothing his forehead. He sucked the air in through his teeth with a hiss, and expelled it again.

'You don't know,' he said finally. 'Your mother has no regard for him at all; I think she'd be angry if I spoke much of him.'

'Tell me,' Martin's appetite was whetted. 'Tell me! I'll keep quiet, I won't let on anything you say.'

'It's your right to know, maybe,' mused Timothy. 'It's a man's birthright to know the ways of his family. But it's not for me to be telling you. You're your mother's son, not mine.'

'Please!' Martin begged, frantic with drink and curiosity. 'You've got to tell me, can't you see?'

Timothy tapped his glass and listened to the accordionist play a lament for Cathal Brugha. He nodded slowly.

'I will, then. If you don't blab.'

'I won't!'

'It'll be our secret, yes? Between us only?'

'I promise, I promise!' Martin said eagerly.

'Very well,' Timothy spoke quietly, beneath the music's insistent notes. 'Your grandfather, my father, Sean Maguire, fought and died for Ireland. The Brits shot him down on a hillside in Fermanagh, and he lies with the heroes in the Republican plot in Armagh.'

Martin felt the impact of each word, opening and shutting his mouth in amazement. He stared silently at Timothy's serious round face, and knew that this was the truth. His world turned upon itself.

'I never knew,' he managed at last. 'I was never told. Never!'

'Your grandmother had a hard time bringing up us children without a man to provide. She never really forgave father for putting country before family.'

Timothy shrugged, fatalistic at the unchanging strangeness of things.

'You see, Martin,' he continued, 'that's the way women think, that's how they're made. The bitterness rubbed off on Mary, and that's how you never were told at all, I suppose.'

'She should have told me,' Martin said, a note of anger in his voice.

'It's a secret, mind,' Timothy said sharply, a little alarmed. 'Not a word!'

'I promised,' agreed Martin, and began to fill with more questions.

They drank more than on any other night spent together in a bar. Irish whiskey with every pint, and a pint on every half-hour, downed to the note of the accordion and the singing.

Towards closing time, a small old man in a dark jacket walked among the patrons in the bar, carrying an unmarked collecting can. He stepped up to Timothy and shook the can gently, so that the coins chinked and clashed inside like bullets dropping into a magazine.

'For the boys,' he said with a wink and a grin. 'For the lads and the great cause. Come on now, dig into your pockets.'

Timothy looked benevolently at the small man and winked drunkenly back at him.

'Sure,' he said in his own Belfast voice, quietly, so as not to slur the words. 'Sure, am I not one of the boys myself?'

'Belfast?' The small man asked, stiffening with sudden respect. 'Are you one of the lads in Belfast then?'

'I am,' said Timothy, 'I am, but I'll say nothing more. You understand.'

He reached and gripped the small man's arm.

'Tell nobody,' he gave another drunken conspiratorial wink.

'God's blessing on you, let me shake that hand,' said the small man fervently. 'God keep you safe and strengthen your arm!'

Martin watched and heard all of this, his mouth opening once more in amazement. He was already in an alcoholic fog, and excitement pumped at his heart, catching at his breath. The small man left, and Timothy looked into his empty glass with a little smile.

'Tim,' said Martin in a hushed voice, 'Tim, are you – ?'

' – I'll say nothing,' said Timothy, but smiled fondly at him. 'And you'll say nothing, either. It's the only way, Martin. The only way.'

He left next day, producing like a conjuror a bottle of perfume from his pocket for Mary. Martin he left with a crackling envelope, and a smiling warning to a wagging finger.

'Don't be opening that till I've gone now, you hear?'

He waved back through the taxi window, and was gone. Martin thought that the tenement flat seemed both empty and smaller without Timothy. Even the six crisp five-pound notes in the envelope could not fill an empty chair, and he did not hear his mother when she said with a shaking of the head: 'He's some talker, that Timothy. A great tale-spinner, he could make a living at it.'

There was a change in Martin, it seemed to Mary. He began to go regularly to mass, even to the men's club in the chapel hall on a Friday night, and Mary was pleased to see him taking his religion more seriously. That was her thought, and wrong.

Martin's interest was not religious. It was Ireland that filled his soul, not God. He listened to the Irish priest, Father O'Cahan, and revelled in the soft brogue and gentle country homilies which studded the old man's ceremony. On Friday nights in the club the talk would turn to the old days in Ireland, days that had become rosier and more entrancing as the years sped from them and they sank back into old men's tales of their youth or of their fathers' day.

Martin listened and was no longer only another unemployed youth. He knew himself to be an exiled child of Ireland, one of the wild geese in a foreign land awaiting the day of return. The older men knew that they would not return, and indeed most had no wish to leave Scotland, but Martin, in the flush of youthful discovery, began to believe that this Ireland of the past lived still, that this Ireland of the cottages and the colleens and the heroes still awaited her exiled children from across the dividing sea.

Martin kept this from his mother, another secret, and a shadow of the secrets he had shared with Timothy. So it was that when the week came which she was to spend in Leeds with her daughter, Mary had no more than the usual mother's doubts as to the wisdom of leaving her son on his own.

She was packed, ready and on the train, and looked again at Martin through the open window of the door.

'Are you sure you'll be all right?'

'I'll be fine, Mum,' Martin hid his impatience at his mother's solicitude. 'I'm twenty next month. I'll be fine.'

'You've got enough money. Remember the paper money,' she raised her voice as the whistle blew shrill along the platform. 'Don't keep that cold pork after tomorrow.'

She leaned awkwardly through the window and Martin kissed her rouged cheek as the train began to move slowly beneath the high glass and iron roof towards the gleaming rails beyond.

'And don't get up to any mischief!' Mary called back.

'I won't, Mum.' Martin waved and stepped back as the train began to bend away from him along the curve of the rail.

'Goodbye, goodbye!' He called and waved, entirely alone for the first time in his life, already tasting the freedom and the pain.

It rained later, long and heavy, the drops sliding like translucent worms across the windows. Martin lifted his eyes above the grey tenements towards the west.

West Belfast was quiet, the storm-lashing rain driving down the stink of the last night's burnings and tear gas. The army had cleared away the fire-blackened debris of cars and lorries hijacked to barricade and burn, and the streets between the rows of terraced houses were wet and cold, with a litter of broken bricks and glass lying here and there to sign the battlegrounds.

The ink ran in blue smudges down the paper when he looked at the scribbled directions. The rain ran straight down the side of the bag and darkened his jeans where they touched.

Martin clutched his anorak tighter at the throat, and picked his way among the jagged fragments of glass beneath a gable end which proclaimed, in foot-high lettering against a background of orange, white and green: 'BRITS OUT! UP THE REPUBLIC!'

He was almost alone on the streets; only a few hurrying souls besides himself braved the torrent from the skies, but behind windows, shadows behind net curtains or in shadows aside from the direct light through the panes, Martin caught glimpses of the motionless watchers who saw him pass.

Dungarvel Street was on the other side of a sudden ugly wasteland of red ash. Martin started across the emptiness, around pools of dark-stained rainwater and past forlorn banks of struggling weeds. A patrol of eight soldiers came sharply along the terrace on the farther side, and Martin told himself that these were the oppressors of his countrymen, but strangely, the words would not take in his mind, and all he really felt was something like disbelief at the sight of these silent running men, dressed in drab green and brown combat gear, and holding ungainly black rifles across their chests. The last two soldiers watched only to the rear, doubling back behind each other to drop and crouch in doorways. As Martin crossed into Dungarvel Street he looked at their white, dirt-streaked faces and saw, with a quickening of disbelief, that a black and dripping rifle muzzle pointed straight at him, and followed his footsteps until the corner took him from its sights.

Martin walked briskly down the street, the tremors in his stomach subsiding, but now even more eager to get indoors and out of the rain. He knocked on Timothy's door. No answer. He knocked again, harder. Again no answer, and with mounting frustration, realizing that Timothy must be out working, he stepped back from the door, glancing up and down the street, turning his head so that the eager rain found its way down inside his collar. From the edge of his vision he saw a corner of the curtain twitch in the neighbour window.

He knocked on that door, twice, before he heard a reluctant voice, an old woman's voice from deep within the hallway.

'Who's that?' The words were quiet as if whispered in the hope that they would not be heard.

'I'm Timothy Maguire's nephew, Martin. He's not in the house, do you know where he'll be?'

'His nephew, do you say?' Frail and suspicious words.

'Yes! Do you know where he is?'

'You might be a nephew, but you're not from here.'

'I'm from Glasgow!' Martin almost shouted with frustration. 'His sister's son, Martin O'Brien!'

'Glasgow.' The old voice hesitated, and relented only a little. 'He'll be working. He's never home before five.'

Martin turned back into the rain and retraced his steps down the street and across the empty waste to a pub he had passed on a corner. Screens of thick wire mesh stretched across the windows like stiff grey nets, with crisp bags and scraps of dirty newspaper caught between the wire and the unwashed glass. The door was narrow and heavy, pitted and scarred like a target.

Inside, the pub was dark, dark and silent, the dim afternoon's light seeping weakly through the windows, and the half-dozen men staring wordlessly at Martin. He pushed back the hood of his anorak, and the rain rolled down his shoulders to the floor, emphasizing the silence with the pattering of the drops breaking upon the floor. The barman raised his eyebrows interrogatively as Martin stepped up to the bar.

'Pint of heavy, please,' Martin put his bag on the floor, and when there were no words in response, he added, 'Terrible wet today.'

'It is,' the barman passed him the full pint glass and held out his hand.

Martin paid, and drank, turning to lean on the bartop. He could see the other men watching him, and he tried a friendly smile and a nod, and the men looked unsmilingly back at him, and then stirred. One, balding and middle-aged in a donkey jacket, walked around Martin and stood at his elbow, between him and the door. Another, younger, perhaps in his late twenties, stroked back his wet black hair and came to lean on the bar in front of Martin, looking him up and down with a thoughtful pursing of his mouth. Martin caught his dark eyes for an instant, and felt uneasy as those eyes slid away across his face and down his length, finally studying the bag at his feet. The young man lifted his head, and looked steadily at Martin.

'Come far?' He had a soft, almost sleepy voice.

'From Glasgow,' Martin replied, then quickly, 'to see my uncle, Timothy Maguire, Dungarvel Street.'

'I thought I recognized the accent. You'll be Scottish, then?'

'I'm Irish by blood. O'Brien. Timothy's my mother's brother.'

'Common enough names, O'Brien and Maguire. But you sound Scottish to me.'

Martin thought he heard a hard edge pushing into the soft voice; a hard edge, a hint of menace, turning towards threat. He could almost feel the man behind staring at him. He began to feel afraid, and swallowed a gulp of beer to steal seconds in which to mask his fear.

'Born and brought up in Glasgow, I suppose I do,' he said at last, and was glad to hear his voice did not tremble.

He lifted his glass and began to drink hastily, to finish and leave. The young man put a hand on his arm.

'Take your time,' he said easily. 'Aren't we just having a wee talk?'

'I'm off to see my uncle.' Martin put down his glass.

'Timothy Maguire? Well, what's a name after all? And this place is thick with the Maguires.'

'What do you mean?' demanded Martin, talking braver than he felt.

'You could pick any name from a phone book, could you not?'

'Look,' Martin bent to pick up his bag. 'I'm over to see my uncle, and I'm going now.'

'You're not,' and the young man gave a slight nod.

The balding man gripped Martin by the arms, and the young man casually gripped his right wrist and turned it outwards, so that his fingers loosened on the handle, and let the bag fall. Martin cursed and struggled, and the balding man slammed him hard against the bar, twice, winding him. He gasped for breath, blinking back tears of pain, and watched his belongings being impatiently scattered on to the bartop. Finally, the young man held the bag upside down and shook it, then let it fall to the floor.

'Nothing,' he said, and looked at Martin. 'Not a thing. Maybe it's the truth.'

'Take no chances, Michael,' said the balding man.

'Do I ever?' asked the young man irritably, and turned to the other men. 'Patrick, keep a look-out. Sean, find this Timothy Maguire, and bring him.'

The men left. Michael studied Martin again and jerked his head towards a corner with a small rickety table and two chairs.

'Put him over there, Peter. Back towards the door.'

Martin was pushed down sharply into the chair. His ribs ached and he touched them gingerly. He was afraid now, thoroughly afraid.

'What's going on?' he asked, speaking in short gasps, catching at his breath. 'What do you want with me?'

'Indeed,' said Michael, and sat opposite him, 'and that's the whole point – what's going on. This is Ireland. There's a war going on, and you fit the wrong way for us to be happy about you strolling in here and chatting about the weather.'

The barman stuffed Martin's clothes back into the bag, and set it on the bartop.

Michael ticked off his fingers in a casual, unexcited manner, like a teacher making something very plain.

'You're Scottish. You've short hair. You're what – twenty, nineteen?'

'Nineteen,' Martin's mouth trembled and he quickly wiped his hand across it to cover his fear.

'Well, all that means one thing only to me.' Michael leaned forward as if to confide. 'Spy. Soldier. Spy.'

'My name's O'Brien! I'm a Catholic!'

'There's plenty Scottish soldiers with Irish names go to mass. And I don't even know your name is O'Brien, now do I?'

'My uncle will tell you!' Martin said quickly. 'Christ, he's one of the lads himself!'

'One of the lads?' mused Michael. 'A brave freedom fighter is he? Well, well.'

The balding man put a hand on Martin's shoulder and squeezed hard, digging his fingers into the sinews behind the collar bone.

'Do we interrogate him?' he said to Michael.

'You're that eager, Peter,' Michael sighed and sat back in the squeaking wooden chair. 'He could be telling us the truth. Well, part of the truth.'

'In which case we'll know,' said the balding man, 'and there could still be time for the other business.'

He took out a cigarette and lit it, drew deeply and then took the cigarette from his mouth and blew on the coal so that it burned redly. He looked at Michael.

'I don't think so,' said Michael. 'Use it to give yourself cancer instead.'

Peter laughed and drew in a breath of smoke. After a little while he gripped Martin's shoulder once more, and dug his fingers even harder, searching for the pain centres. Martin stood it for a short while, then the hard fingers sent an agonizing spasm through his shoulder and arm. He twisted away and reached up to massage his shoulder.

'Did that hurt?' asked Peter.

'Yes.' Martin felt hatred coming behind the fear.

'Well that's a little indication,' said Peter. 'If you're not what you say you are, that pain will be like a nothing.'

'Leave him alone,' said Michael sharply. 'Violence is a tool, not a pleasure.'

'God, Michael,' Peter grinned maliciously. 'Aren't you becoming the intellectual?'

'You shut up,' said Michael. 'Do you hear me? Shut up!'

Martin listened, and the Ireland of the tales suffocated and died inside him.

Timothy came at last, dressed in his overalls, his face pale and sweating and trying to smile. Michael looked him up and down thoughtfully, as he had earlier inspected Martin.

'Well,' he said finally. 'I know you, Maguire, and you know me. You're no danger to us, or to the enemy. Who's this boy?'

'My nephew, Martin.' Timothy was subdued.

'I'm not sure, Maguire, and I don't take chances. He looks like one of those bloody-minded Scots soldiers to me.'

'He's only a boy!' Timothy took a pace forward.

'I've got boys of his age dying out there,' said Michael evenly, 'and so have the Brits.'

He stood up and walked to stand only a foot away from Timothy, looking levelly into his eyes. Martin saw Timothy turn even paler and look away, down at the floor, shuffling his feet a little.

'Your nephew is under the impression, Maguire, that you're a bold Fenian man, a freedom fighter, one of the lads.'

'Him?' Peter laughed. 'The most he could fight would be a full glass.'

'No, no, a mistake!' Timothy licked his lips. 'I've the greatest respect for you, and I pay my contributions with the best, but I'd never claim your glory for myself! No, never!'

'I should hope you would not,' said Michael, and his eyes did not move from Timothy's face. 'I'm fighting a revolutionary war, and there's enough trouble for us all, without the need to enforce discipline on such as you.'

He put a hand into his jacket pocket, and brought out a blue steel revolver. Timothy stiffened, licking his lips again. Martin could almost feel his fear; almost smell his terror. Michael tapped Timothy on the elbow with the revolver barrel.

'You take my meaning?' he asked, and put the gun back in his pocket.

Timothy nodded, making small stuttering noises, blinking rapidly.

'Like I said,' Michael continued, 'I'm fighting a revolutionary war, and you've never even thrown a bloody brick, let alone been on active service!'

'My father died for Ireland!' said Timothy hoarsely.

'Sure,' said Michael with contempt. 'Is that not your style? Another man's deeds again!'

'I'll make it up to you for your trouble, I will!'

'Oh, you will,' agreed Michael. 'You'll be hearing from us. Now, get out, the pair of you.'

Martin stood up, and Peter tossed his bag at him, hard, using both hands, as if throwing a medicine ball.

'You're a lucky boy. Michael's getting soft!'

'Enough of that!' Michael rounded on him. 'Save your criticisms for the proper time, not here!'

He turned back to Timothy and Martin, still standing without moving.

'I said, get out!' And he turned to the bar and unbidden the barman placed a pint in his hand.

Timothy and Martin walked awkwardly down the street, silence between them. The rain had stopped, and grey clouds swept overhead like tattered banners.

'Come on, we'll go up to the house,' said Timothy at last.

'No,' said Martin. 'I don't want to stay, not after that.'

'They won't trouble you again, Martin,' Timothy spread his hands, 'don't judge us by that!'

'Us?' Martin sneered, and stopped walking, to look at his uncle. 'Us? What's this "us"? You've never thrown a brick, remember?'

A car drove past with the slow speed of a hearse, the passenger gazing out the side window at them. Martin wondered what work they were engaged upon.

'If I'd known you were coming!' Timothy pleaded. 'Martin, you must see, you just got in the way.'

'Do you never wonder who else "just got in the way"? Is that how the cause is won?'

'Martin, Martin! You're upset, and I don't blame you. Come on up to the house, at least for the night, and I'll drive you to Larne tomorrow.'

'No, I'm going,' Martin looked up and down the street for the way out of the terraces and back to the railway station.

'Martin, please. Don't let us part like this.'

Martin looked stiffly past, and Timothy sighed and looked down at his shoes and the wet pavement. There was silver creeping into his hair, and a thinning begun at the crown of his head. Martin felt a new emotion: pity.

'Well, just for tonight, then,' he said, and saw Timothy lift his head and smile a growing shadow of his old beaming smile.

That evening, while Timothy cooked, whistling with his jauntiness mostly restored by a large whiskey, Martin looked out the window at the huddled row of terraced houses opposite, on the other side of the twilight street. A puddle caught the light from the window in a lonely splash of illumination, and he thought with longing of tall grey tenements in the rain.

THE GREAT McGUNNIGLE
Edward Boyle

It was the start of a new term at St Andrew's High School in Wellshaw, the grey Lanarkshire steel manufacturing town. As his parents were still on holiday and he had no gentle mother's hand to stir him in the morning, young Milloy had set the radio alarm for 7.45. He awoke with the voice of Terry Wogan announcing an old number by the Seekers, 'The Carnival Is Over', and indeed for Alex, the carnival was over, the holidays were over, seven weeks of bliss were about to give way to many months of worry. Eyelids still heavy, his first conscious thought was of school and the dawning realization that he might again have that big swine, McGunnigle, for English.

'Surely,' he thought, 'I'll not have McGunnigle this year.' Milloy was starting his fifth term at school and in his previous year had the ultimate misfortune to meet up with McGunnigle, the bane of his life. In his first, second and third years he had been lucky enough not to have drawn the great big toerag, for there were 1,100 pupils and fourteen teachers in the English department. In fourth year with the odds the same, he and McGunnigle had met up and for the first time Milloy hated school, all because of that one hulking brute, all five feet eleven of him. Now the odds had shortened and with only 380 pupils taking Higher English, the chances of getting McGunnigle again were all the more likely. But perhaps the fates would be kinder this time.

Several times the previous year, Milloy had felt like packing it up. On one occasion, after a last period altercation with McGunnigle, he had come home in so obviously distraught a state that his mother had asked what was wrong. Ordinarily, Milloy did not tell of what went on in school unless it was something unconnected with the classroom like a parents' meeting or a school function such as a PT dance or a Fayre. This time he had almost burst into tears and at his mother's insistence, told of his misery. She had been aghast but felt that there was little she could do to help her son. She recalled earlier occasions when Alex was subjected to bullying at his primary school, that interviewing headmistress and staff had helped little. In truth, she like many parents, felt out of her depth visiting a school, whether the corridors were bustling at breaks or quiet during classes. Neither mother nor son would confide in father, a security van driver, who was able to look after himself and thought his son should be capable of doing the same.

Strangely enough, the worst confrontations between pupil and teacher had not been in class but at several school functions. Milloy had brought to a Hallowe'en party a girlfriend, Greta, who had to suffer close attention from McGunnigle racing across the floor to grab her several times and get her to dance with him, Milloy looking on in silent rage. At the tea interval Greta whispered to her partner that she could smell drink off McGunnigle and that when they were dancing he ran his fingers down the length of her spine. When next McGunnigle made an approach, Milloy intervened, there was a short flurry, not enough to attract general attention, thanks to the nearby presence of two teachers who separated the would-be adversaries. On the way home when Greta aired her grievances, Milloy ground his teeth and silently swore that one day he would flatten McGunnigle, no matter the consequences.

Another vexation was when Mrs Milloy was helping with the 'White Elephant' stall at the annual school fête. During its two hours' duration, McGunnigle had hardly quit the vicinity, staring at Mrs Milloy minutes at a time, and offering derisory sums of money for displayed items. Near the end of the sale he had put down ten pence for an indoor TV aerial and wanted to take a small dainty hedgehog pincushion for five pence. 'Sure no one will come and buy that now,' he leered, 'the sale's nearly over!' Mrs Milloy ignored him and bought the pincushion for the asking price of one pound.

Further wranglings occurred in class, mainly accusations over homework, copying in exams, inattention and dumb insolence.

'You did this homework in the bog by the look of it.'

'You copied chunks of this essay out of the *Reader's Digest*.'

'How come you and Wilson here have the same answers?'

Almost every day Milloy could expect trouble from McGunnigle and almost every day Milloy felt like walking out of school. During that summer vacation, his mother had tried to comfort him. 'Perhaps you won't get him in fifth year. Remember that this is a short term for fifth year. The Highers begin at the end of April and you won't see him when the exams are over. Try to be patient for you don't want to do anything foolish at this stage and ruin your career.' Milloy listened to her but was not comforted. An inner voice told him that he would be fated to meet up with McGunnigle this term and short one or not, it would be hell.

It was all so unfair; he was but five feet eight in height, weighed eight stone eleven pounds and had never been all that strong and active; his only claim to athletic prowess had been at primary school when the football team had been short of a player, the teacher had picked him blindly from among the few pupils who turned up to watch the match; he was quite fast and played as a nippy winger, avoiding physical contact as far as possible. McGunnigle was nearly six feet tall, scaled ten stone ten pounds and was active in school sports; Milloy watched him enviously in the gym, climbing ropes, somersaulting over the horse and playing basketball at which with his height he was easily the leading goal snatcher. In the annual Teachers v Pupils soccer game, McGunnigle and Milloy were both playing with Milloy coming off worse; his opponent was playing 'sweeper' and had twice swept Milloy on to the surrounding cinder track thereby causing an annoying gravel rash on both knees. These his mother had tenderly bathed and bound, again saying nothing to her husband.

That sunny August morn he rolled reluctantly out of bed to face the oncoming day. He made breakfast from the cornflakes and eggs that his mother had provided. Lunch he could get at school and evening dinner at his aunt's down the road. It was an easy ten minutes' walk to school, a journey however he did not enjoy for he was apt to meet McGunnigle who lived in the same area and would cross the road or bring his brisk walk to a dawdle if he saw his tormentor in the distance. There would however be no chance of an encounter that particular day as pupils and teachers did not meet one another until ten o'clock on opening day.

Later with pounding heart he saw the timetables and class lists. To his horror but not to his surprise, he had McGunnigle for English. The only consolation and small consolation at that was the class met for four double and one single period per week and this was not one of the days. All he could hope for now was that something drastic would happen to McGunnigle; perhaps his father, an electrical engineer, would emigrate to Australia or South Africa in response to one of those alluring newspaper advertisements; perhaps he would break a leg, or better still, his neck, when doing one of his handsprings in the gym; or perhaps . . .

But that term was to run its fateful course. With the first meeting of the class, Milloy could feel the old tension as though there had been no intervening holidays, and he could sense McGunnigle's sardonic gaze upon him even when the class was busy working. The class was well aware of the situation and waited, part in hope, part in trepidation, for the outbreak of hostilities. But open war did not occur immediately, probably because there is a feeling of freshness and light at the start of a new term; the building is clean and smelling of fragrant disinfectant, the floors are gleaming, the walls scrubbed free of graffiti, shining blackboards and desks inviting renewed effort, the windows repaired and all intact. Unfortunately as the freshness evaporates the old animosities reappear, and so was it with Milloy and McGunnigle.

Three weeks and twenty-seven periods later, the inevitable occurred and it sprang from the old source; accusations of slovenly work at home and class, copying, inattention and insolence. Fundamentally Milloy was peace-loving and exercised great patience in face of provocation, trying to go about his work ignoring the other's presence, keeping, as it were, to his own side of the arena. It was actually homework that caused the final break.

'I don't remember getting your last homework.'

'What homework was that?'

'The appreciation of Cowper.'

'Y'mean Davie Cooper? Y'could hardly expect me to write an appreciation of an ex-Rangers player.'

'Don't be smart.'

31

'Oh, I'm not Smart, he's in 5c.'

That was it. Milloy could take no more and all restraint vanished. But he was conscious of his disadvantage in height and weight and knew that if he went in with bare fists, he would never get within arm's length of the swine. Instinctively he remembered a weapon close at hand, the board ruler. It lay conveniently projecting over the teacher's desk, five feet long, six inches broad, solid oak with sharp edge. He grabbed, advanced a few feet between desks, crashed it down on his adversary's head and, when he put up his hands for protection, brought the ruler in a full force arc on his fingers. McGunnigle screamed; Milloy shivered in elation. In utter silence the class stared with unbelieving eyes and only after a few seconds broke into a babble of sighs, jeers and cheers, just as dismissal bell rang.

Milloy dropped his weapon and stumbled from the room, a thin smile of satisfaction on his face.

'That's it,' he thought to himself, 'that's it at last and I don't give a damn if that's the last of me and St Andrew's. It was worth it, bloody well worth it.'

He was in the toilet splashing his face with water when Hoban, the Deputy Rector, touched his shoulder.

'The Head wants to see you in his room.'

Milloy nodded and dried his hands and face with a paper towel. Curious eyes, some friendly, some hostile, watched his progress on the two minute walk across the school to the Head's study. Milloy, still flushed, knocked timidly and the green light above the door blinked, bidding him enter. The Rector who was looking out the window turned grim-faced to confront Milloy.

'Well . . . this is a serious business and I don't see what I can do to help you. I can't keep it within the school. Assaulting a pupil is a police matter, Mr Milloy.'

FIRST FOOT
Janice Galloway

It was the sun nearly woke me this morning. One minute I'm asleep and the next I'm awake and staring at the clock. It says five to eight so I've had a good sleep. I'm lying back congratulating myself on it when I notice how light the room is, even through the curtains. First sunny day of the New Year, I think. Has to be a good sign.

I can still hear Mammy thumping about in the living-room, putting the divan up, transforming it with sleight of cushions into a settee again. I hold my breath and listen, but there's still no telling what sort of mood she's in. It's a sort of neutral thumping about. I stretch out full, tipping the head-and-foot-board at once and grinning at the ceiling, then sling my legs over the edge of the bed to sit up, still listening. It does seem a wee bit more noisy than usual right enough. Taking a bit of a risk, I think. Maybe wake up the gorgon. And that decides it.

I hate being in when my sister gets up. We *don't get on*, that is to say we hate the sight of each other. I mean it too – we've both been working on it a long time, as far back as I can remember (and probably before that on her side). With me, it's fear. She hates me because she thinks everything I do is specially designed to get at her. For example, I don't smoke/she gets through forty a day; I wake up early/she sleeps till noon; I like peace and quiet/she likes perpetual telly. I'm sixteen. She's thirty-seven. I sometimes think that last bit is the crux of the whole thing. That, and my passivity. I'm really wet. When she hits me, she knows I won't hit her back and it makes her worse, like she thinks I'm trying to prove I'm better than her or something. And I'm not. Irene is unpredictable and vicious with it. I'm just scared sick.

On top of that, she hates mornings. She treats them with a fierce spite, and I'm not going to get in the way of that, not with the day being so nice as well. I'm going to get up and go for Joseph. Maybe go for a walk on the shore front, down the shops, buy a magazine. Just so long as it's out.

So I get up and I go for a wash. As soon as I turn the taps on, Mammy shouts through for me not to use up all the hot water, then I hear her putting the kettle on to make me a cup of tea. I think about shouting back for her not to bother – but I don't mind. I'm safe enough for ten minutes or so anyway.

I put on the clothes still lying about the floor from the night before: saves me thinking and saves me getting a row about leaving the place a mess. I push the curtains to one side while I'm doing up my shirt and there's the sun. It really is glorious. One of those clear, nippy days right at the start of the year when you think you can see into the middle of next week and the colours are really sharp. Wee blades of grass out the back coated with frost and next door's washing still on the line, totally stiff like cardboard. And there's this cartoon picture in my head, somebody sawing the washing off the line and bashing it with a hammer to fold it – just daft things making me laugh and the sky pure blue and completely cloudless.

Not much of a laughing mood in the kitchenette, though. Just Mammy standing at the window in her dressing-gown and slippers. She hands the mug over without looking at me. Then she says: 'It's you should be making me breakfast, never mind the other way round.'

She sometimes gets like that in the mornings, especially at holidays. Third of January already, but the haar of the New Year still hangs on round the house. She turns her back to clatter about making toast and things, muttering about ingratitude. It's the way she's woken up, and I can feel my face miserable in spite of myself. I can't stay in with this, I think. It's going to get me down and I know what happens after that. I get myself into a depression and that makes Mammy worse and then Irene gets up out of her bed like the thing from the black lagoon . . . I'm for off while I've got the chance.

So I sneak on my duffel and get my bag. Quiet. It's always important not to give the game away that I know what's coming for some reason. I try to keep my voice chirpy, but it comes out sort of flat, sort of underhand. 'I'm away out.' And while I'm drawing the door off the snib, gently so as not to wake Irene up,

Mammy appears suddenly, her face hanging, at the top of the lobby.

'Where are you away to already?'

'Joe's.' I'm stalling. Then she sighs. I can hear it all the way down the lobby.

'Will you be home for your tea?'

There's a funny edge about her voice. She's really upset about something and I can see it all over her face. But I don't know what she wants me to say.

'You tell me nothing. Will you not even be in for your tea?' Her breathing is funny as well.

There's me at the other end of the lobby, feeling guilty, but I haven't a clue what I've done and I don't know how to make it better. I know she sometimes resents me going out all the time, but she just moans if I stay in. So I squirm for a minute and grab the compromise: 'Aye, okay. Okay, I'll be in for my tea,' and I shut the door fast, desperate to get out in the fresh air. I stand for a minute at the door, just breathing it in with my eyes shut.

Joe's still in his bed when I get to his place. I've to wake him up by chapping on the window and pulling faces in at him. One of the cats gets up on the window-sill when it sees me and we both climb in the window together, me laughing and calling Joe a lazy so-and-so and the cat rubbing itself like crazy off his ankles and purring for something to eat; Joe smiling away in the middle of it.

Joe's great: really good-natured. I don't think I've ever seen him lose his temper. Every other day I get him up out of bed and he just smiles and gets me something to drink and we have breakfast together. I think the house has something to do with it. He lives in this big house on the shore front and more or less on his own. His mother (a widow, like mine) stays out a lot, sometimes for days on end; and his brother's so quiet you wouldn't even know he was there half the time – he sort of tiptoes about the place. Or goes out, too. So Joe gets the run of the place; him and the three cats and the rabbit. Oh – and the tropical fish. He's been buying these tropical fish recently and he can sit and stare at them for hours. Some nights we get in a takeaway and just sit in his room watching the fish and eating the food and talking till we fall asleep. And even then, it's still me wakes him up in the morning.

Anyway, Joe's in the house by himself this morning. He fixes some grub for us and the cats, then we're out for a walk. Not that we do much or go very far: just down the rocks to look for anemones, beachcomb along the sand till we get cold. We go up the town after that and buy two cups of coffee at the Melbourne to warm our hands off them and get hysterical at the man telling us it's time we were married. He says that every time we go in there. We keep telling him we're not going out or anything, just friends, and it doesn't make any difference. I don't know whether he doesn't believe us or whether it's just a good joke for him. Joe's mother certainly doesn't think it's a joke. She's always getting on about me seeing him all the time, and wasn't it time I got myself a *proper boyfriend* and I should stop staying overnight because I'd *get a name about myself.* Joe gets really grim when she does that. It's as if they don't want us to be friends or something. Or probably don't believe that's all there is to it. Dirty minds.

We stay in there a long time, blethering. The man gives us another cup of coffee for nothing because we stay in so long and asks us what on earth we find to talk about. I couldn't tell him. It's everything and nothing. We just sort of spark each other off and we never seem to get bored with each other. This time, we're talking about the look on my mother's face this morning, but we shut up when the man comes over. Joe gets back to it after the coffee arrives, speaking and stirring with the spoon, 'She's likely just fed up,' he says. 'Just wanting you to talk to for a change. Maybe she's lonely.'

I say nothing.

'It's just not in her to ask you to stay in, either. She wants you to want to stay in.'

Now I know he's right. But I also know, and he does too, that it isn't in *me* to stay in while Irene's there. Holidays are murder.

We've finished the second cups now and Joe's up to buy a quarter of sweeties. We walk from one end of Dockhead Street to the other eating them, then back up again. Most of the shops are still closed for the New Year but it doesn't matter: we've hardly any money anyway. We're just looking. And we keep blethering the whole time. We end up back at his place with more warm coffee, staring out at the waterfront from the bay window and still talking and stroking the cats. I'm really mellow by this time, with the water and the brightness of the day and the feel of the cats' fur under our hands – full of that nice, relaxed sort of tiredness you get after a long walk. I'm happy. Then I look at my watch. My face is sliding while I'm standing up.

'I said I'd go back for my tea. I better shift.'

But he knows I'm not wanting to and he knows fine why. I keep looking out the window for a wee bit, holding on to it before I have to let go.

'I'll be away then.'

And all the time he knows perfectly well I'm dreading it, and the good time we were having isn't making it any easier. It's making it worse. I'm hoping he's going to offer to walk me back or something, then suddenly his face lights up.

'I'll come round and be your first foot! Bet that would cheer your mother up. We'll buy a bottle of that stuff she likes, take some shortbread, do the thing right . . . ' And he's off into the kitchen hunting up money and biscuit tins. I'm pretty taken with the idea. Mammy likes Joe, he can make a difference to her. And the daftness of the first foot thing will make us all laugh. We'll have a present for her as well: she'll say we shouldn't have but she'll be pleased all the same. It gets better and better as I think about it.

Outside, we count up the rest of Joe's Christmas money and the dregs of my cash – enough for a half bottle of advocaat and a wee jar of cocktail cherries, for a touch of celebration. But it takes us ages to find someplace that'll sell us the drink. Bloody hell, I think, it's only advocaat. Mammy isn't too happy with drink in the house, but she does like this stuff – it doesn't count. Especially when you mix it up with lemonade. They call it a snowball and you can even give it to weans, for goodness' sake. We were giggling all the way up the road about it. I'm all warm and excited by this time, really happy inside and looking forward to springing the surprize. Me and my best friend; taking our good time and bringing it home in triumph for my mammy to share. She's always saying life doesn't give her many laughs, but when it does, she knows how to enjoy them. She's great fun when she's in the mood. And here's me bringing luck to the house with the first foot and the bottle. O aye, I'm looking forward to it.

The sight of the front door calms me down a bit, though. Irene, I think. She's been murder for the past two days and I can't afford to give her any excuse. She doesn't like me bringing folk in the house – and she doesn't like Joe. Still, no problem. We can go in the kitchenette and wait, then Mammy will come through to see what's keeping me. Fine, we can wait in there and have the drinks ready for her coming through.

I push open the door gently, shouting, 'It's me,' at the closed living-room and the two of us sneak into the kitchenette. I start looking for the glasses and Joe gets the tissue paper off the wee bottle. He's still laughing when she comes through. She just stands there in the door with her face deadly and me with my smile frozen and stuck in place.

'Where the hell have you been?'

And I just stand rooted. I'm getting dizzy.

'Where the hell were you? You said you'd be home for your tea. I had it ready for you ages ago. It's over there, cold and dry as dust. And you'll bloodywell eat it if it chokes ye. Good money wasted.'

Her face is really bitter. She's noticed Joe and flinches a bit with being so angry in front of him, but that doesn't stop it. And the violence of it knocks the stuffing out of me and everything I wanted to say.

Joe fumbles in: 'She's been at my place, Mrs Galloway, we've been – '

But she's too mad to listen. She's shouting: 'Well take her back there then. On ye go. Never want to be in here anyway; quick as ye can get out in the mornings. On ye go. Get out of my sight. Away with your friends: let them feed ye.' Her whole body is trembling.

I'm trapped with my own speechlessness. I'm wanting to yell, to make her see. I want her to notice the bottle we've brought. And she does see it, but only with her eyes. It still doesn't mean anything to her – just a bottle on the table and a jar of daft cherries. I want her to really see it, recognize it for what I mean it to be – some kind of a token and some sort of prayer it's impossible to speak out loud in this damned house. I want her to see all that at once and stop, take it and pour it out and drink hopefully to the New Year; to accept it. Accept *me*. It's not just a bloody drink I've brought her – I'm trying to tell her I love her. But I know she's too blind and too angry. And I know who's done the blinding. Irene.

I want to scream, but I know I won't. I never do. Instead, I just burn with guilt, shame and self-disgust.

I'd been stupid. I should have known what my sister could do when my back was turned. Then her voice floats in, sickly sweet, from the living-room. 'Don't upset yourself with her, Mammy. Just come away through. Leave her with her "friend".' And my mother just turns her heel and goes.

Me and Joe just stand in the kitchenette. He doesn't speak, he's waiting, afraid for what I might do. Then I feel the tears starting down my face and I run to hide in the bedroom, just stand and stare at the frozen washing still on the line outside. My jaw hurts with biting it down: *Mammy, don't listen to her, help me to find the words for once.* But it goes on hurting and I know I won't say it. I know I won't ever say it.

Staring, cursing our weakness, I make up my mind, *Let her win.*

I start gathering my things together.

A PICTURE OF ZOE
Liam Stewart

I've got a picture of Zoe. I've still kept it after a year. It's a drawing by the Artist, and there he is now, near where I'm sitting, still sketching away trying to make a living.

The old lady approved of Zoe the first minute she saw her. It was the look of her for a start, all bright and clean on the grimy street, with the blonde hair bouncing about like a shampoo advert. I could see that look in the old lady's eyes when she met us going to her work that day. They're roaming over the details, impressed, storing them up for later reference: the spotless creamy coat, the shiny mauve high heels (not too high), the matching shoulder-bag and the black skirt made of that good quality material. And when Zoe opened her mouth, that was it! The old lady's over the moon! Zoe's well-spoken. The Bearsden accent set the seal on what the old lady saw as a very nice little package.

The old lady herself has always had this thing about talking properly: saying 'you' instead of 'yous', things like that. She's not that good at it herself, but she admires folk that can do it. It's all because she thinks she's a cut above this area. She even wears chiffon scarves and puts on red nail polish to go out to her cleaning job. Glamour girl at 48. It's a bit pathetic, if you could see it.

When I got back home to the scheme that night, she's sitting by the fire in her dressing-gown, drinking coffee and puffing a fag, still smirking to herself even though it's a sad picture on the telly.

'My! That's a nice girl, son!' she says, taking a sip of her coffee and winking at me. 'Where did you meet her?'

She knew it must have been somewhere good. Not the bus queue or the social security or the chippie or anywhere in this dump, with the boarded-up houses and the packs of scabby dogs marauding through the closes and over the waste ground. Oh no!

She could see at a glance Zoe had never picked her way through this terrain.

Zoe was a college girl. Dunky had this girlfriend that was training to be a teacher, and Zoe was her pal. So one night Zoe and me met up along with Dunky and the girlfriend. That was how it all started, a sort of blind date. I was told afterwards that she thought I was a nice-looking boy. Actually, she wasn't the first to hold this opinion and, I have to admit, apart from everything else about her, she had her curves in the right places. So the old animal attraction was there all right. But it struck me pretty soon that, for somebody who was going to be a teacher, Zoe knew less about the real world than the old lady's budgie. Everything was 'gorgeous' (with the head cocked on one side) or 'awful' (with the eyes aghast).

For me, it was a bit of a laugh at first going out with somebody who talked like Zoe. To the mates, when they found out about it, it was me going out with a pure snob. I often wondered what Zoe was thinking about those first few times we went out. It was hard to know. If I looked at her quickly, before she had time to flick on the old smile, and caught her in one of those quizzical glances she thought I didn't notice, it looked as though she regarded me as from another species, one of the lower orders who might give her some useful material for one of her school projects.

And God! Was she out of touch! I don't know where she usually went, but sometimes when I was out with her she seemed to be looking about herself as if she thought there was Apaches up every close. And her mouth was pursed so tight you would have thought there was something putrid in the atmosphere.

That's the way it looked that first time at The Happy Moon Chinese restaurant in the Dumbarton Road. I thought I better play a strong card as an opener – a good night out, a good meal. I had been to this particular grub shop before, with Dunky and Tam, and it had not been too bad at all.

Well, as soon as I step over the threshold with Zoe I can see it isn't such a high-class establishment as it seemed the last time. After drifting along the street breathing in Zoe's perfume, the smell of stale fat is too noticeable. Zoe's eyes are darting about as if I've brought her to an opium den in Hong Kong, and though she makes a big effort to keep nattering and flashing the old teeth, I can see she's ill at ease in such shabby surroundings. She takes in the shortcomings of the place and so do I: the carpet worn in patches through to the backing, the yellow stains like big suns on the table-cloth and, next to the kitchen door on the green flock wallpaper, a big mark that looks like a blotch of blood or where somebody has flung a plate of something they weren't satisfied with. It's dimly lit right enough, but the only other customers are an old couple who look like a pair of dossers and keep staring over at us out of their shadowy corner.

But it was what happened when we were in the middle of our dinner (quite a nice wee chicken chow mein that I think she was even beginning to enjoy) that really put the tin-lid on it. This drunk guy staggers in, unnoticed as it happens, and sinks down at the table next to us. I can see Zoe stiffening and leaning away from him. The guy's head's rolling about, but somehow or other he manages to convey his order, and a minute later a bowl of chicken noodle soup (the burn-the-mouth kind we've just had) is plunked down in front of him, with the flowery china spoon. But by this time he has begun to nod off to sleep. His arms have slipped down over the sides of his chair and his head is sagging down towards his chicken noodle. Down he goes till his nose makes contact with the soup. It scalds him enough to jerk him a foot up and almost open his heavy lids. Then he droops down again, the nose dips into the chicken noodle and he jerks up again. And so it goes on, like one of those pecking toys or as if there's a spring in his spine. By this time he has an audience. It's an entertainment to the old pair chomping away in their corner, and the waiter and manager are standing watching, arms folded, jabbering away in Chinese. The upward jerks are reduced to about four inches now, whether because the guy's sinking into a deeper sleep or his nose is getting acclimatized, I don't know. But the Chinese boys obviously see a danger that the soup might get spilled or our pecking friend might get drowned, so the manager strides over and whips the bowl out from under the guy's nose. He shakes him for about twenty seconds and then shoves a bill into his hand, jabbering away the whole time. Obviously he's telling him to cough up for the soup and then get out. The guy slumps back in his chair, holding the bill out at arm's length, trying to read it through his drunken stupor.

In his state it might as well be in Cantonese, but vaguely the aggro of the situation begins to dawn on him and he goes into a Clint Eastwood act. He crumples the bill and drops it on the floor, trying to stare at The Happy Moon boys the whole time. Then he points his finger at the manager.

'You're at it,' he says slowly, ' . . . I've been oot in India.'

There's no answer to that. You have to laugh. But, Christ, the manager dives straight into the argument and the waiter backs him up. This is not India, they're shouting, and quoting him the price of chickens and the upkeep of The Happy Moon and asking him when he was in India anyway.

However, the chicken noodle guy then decides to be magnanimous. He holds up his hand, dismissing the argument, and heaves himself on to his feet, just about cowping the table in the process. He's standing there rocking about as if he's on a ship, digging deep into the pockets of his baggy blue suit. They're scrabbling about picking up sauce bottles and straightening the table.

'Right, now,' he asks contemptuously, counting the pile of change he's dug out, 'how much is your soup?'

But it transpires he hasn't got enough, so they waive the bill and start huckling him out the door. This could have been a very bad move because the guy breaks free and starts to swear at them. But at the last minute they have the sense to hold back and let him do a dusting-off routine and tell them, as he stumbles out the door, that he'll never eat in The Happy Moon again and neither will his friends and he'll ruin them. They're clearing his table when the door swings open again and he steps back in. I knew it.

'Your soup was shitey, anyhow!' he says, gives them the V-sign and falls back through the door.

It's a riveting scene. I keep my eyes on the door for a couple of seconds to see if he'll do another encore, and then I look at Zoe. Her eyes are wide.

'How awful!' she says. 'That poor man looked as though he could have done with a bowl of soup.'

Poor man! A bowl of soup! Christ! The guy looked as if he'd been pouring booze down his throat the whole day. But I can see an expression on Zoe's face that tells me she really thinks it was a distasteful incident. So, at the bus stop, I say to her that I am sorry that her evening had been spoiled.

'Oh don't be silly, Gerry!' she says, giving me a peck on the cheek. 'Really! It was a lovely meal,' and she flashes the smile, maybe just a bit less bright than usual.

That was Zoe – Queen of the Bearsden soup-kitchen. But the trouble was, and Glasgow being what it is, when she was out with me she came much closer to the unwashed orders than any meals-on-wheels Bearsden lady might ever have desired. No car you see. It had to be buses and walking in the city streets, and going to much lower-class places than it seemed she was used to.

So the next time we ventured out for something to eat, I decided to take her somewhere in the centre of the town. As usual, she says she's easy where we go, so I suggest The South Pacific. It's quite a good eating shop, a cut above the usual Wimpy Bar type places and it's licensed. It's self-service right enough, but the haddock and chips is always good and they give you a big helping. Everything's going very smoothly in fact, until we come into contact with the Artist. This is an old guy who always carries a drawing-pad about with him and a row of pencils in the top pocket of his jacket. He gives you that impression somehow of a boy who gambled at one time, but never quite made it. He's always unshaven and he wears a soft, brown hat with greasy stains on the brim. There's one or two places in the town where he's allowed to come into your company and ask if you want a charcoal sketch of yourself for a pound. The South Pacific is one of these places. Now, I had seen him doing his routine before, but, of course, had always given him the knock-back myself, never having had a pound to spare. But anyway, he's there that day and he homes in on me and Zoe and, of course, it's Zoe he wants to sketch. So she gives him the smile and we say go ahead.

He's rabbiting away the whole time as he does the sketch with what looks like an ordinary school pencil with the Green Cross

Code on it. Then he comes with the line, 'Now what colour are your eyes, my dear?', looking into Zoe's eyes. 'Ah yes, a lovely blue,' he says, taking out his blue pencil and colouring in the eyes. He does the same with his red one for the lips. Seeing it upside down, I'm not impressed, and when he hands it over I can see, and I'm no art critic, that it's a joke – something maybe a kid of seven would do. He's just drawn an oval in a hard line, added basic eye, nose and mouth shapes, scribbled on a few squiggles for the hair and then coloured in the eyes and lips, and that's it. It's humanoid. It could be anybody.

'Do you not see yourself like that, dear? Well, there you are. That's the way the Artist sees you.'

His patter's terrible. I feel like telling him to get lost, but Zoe might think I'm too tight to pay the pound so I give him it. Zoe smiles and thanks him. The Artist tips his greasy hat and slides out the seat to look for some other sucker. I turn and see Zoe looking down her nose at the paper in her hand, as if she thinks it's an insult.

'It's not really very good,' I say casually, 'you don't have to keep it.'

'Oh no! It's lovely, Gerry! Really! Honest! It was really sweet of you to pay for it.' She puts it away carefully in her bag.

And that's the way it went on. Whenever Zoe and me walked through the town, we seemed to draw these people like magnets: the tramps and the winos and the hard-luck merchants. Zoe would rummage in the mauve handbag and out would come the purse and she would flash the old smile and give them the hand-out, like one of those ladies in the old days giving alms to the needy. It was a bit embarrassing, to tell you the truth. However, we still went out together. There was still the animal attraction, as I said, though, mind you, things were going a bit slow in that direction and I wasn't sure why. One thing that was always on my mind was that she had never invited me out to the Bearsden homestead, which I thought might have been a better bet than the scheme with the old lady sitting smoking at the fire.

One night, after we had been going out for about two months, I had a dream about Zoe – one of those erotic dreams. It was nice at first. You know the kind. The two of us splashing about naked underneath a waterfall in a beautiful sunny hollow – Walt Disney for adults. Then we're getting dressed and I overhear her saying on the phone (this is back in the beach-house or the log cabin or somewhere), 'I can't speak now, Nigel. I'm still with the tramp.' I'm blazing mad and just about to confront her . . . and that's all I remember of the dream.

A dream always makes you think. It gives you a strange feeling. I'm sitting toasting my toes by the fire and sipping my coffee. It's waterfalls outside and I don't want to go. I just want to sit here and try to think about the dream and see how it feels.

'Remember you've got to sign on,' the old lady says from the other side of the fire, waking me out of my day-dream. 'Are you still going out with that nice girl, son?' she asks, taking a big drag on her fag. 'When are you going to bring her home for her tea?'

She's winking again. I mutter something and scuttle through to the bedroom to get dressed. Bring her here? Oh no! I've had enough of Zoe's hollow smiles at me and my patch. Bringing her home to the old lady's fawning patter just would not do. No way. I can imagine the old lady curtseying or something and skelping the chair with a duster before Zoe put her bum on it.

What with that dream that wouldn't stop going round in my head, and the grey rain drizzling down all day and something funny in Zoe's voice on the phone last night, I wasn't looking forward to seeing her that night. I was to meet her outside the Odeon at eight, so I decided to have a couple of drinks first – just to get out of the rain and stay away from the old lady.

I drift into Lauder's in Sauchiehall Street at about six. As usual it's mobbed, vibrating with the juke-box. There's nobody I know so it's pleasant enough to stand at the bar, letting the bitter taste of a pint of Guinness soothe my worries, relaxing in the anonymity of the crowd. It engulfs you – the noise, the colours, the smell of the drink and the perfume. I get another pint of Guinness and find a corner to sit and read my paper. We're getting Jim Reeves from the old juke-box now – 'You're the only good thing'.

The customary perusal of the Situations Vacant: sales reps mostly. 'Do you want to make 25,000 a year? You can if you're the right sort of bloke.'

I know I'm the wrong sort, so I fold the paper over to the crossword. This is one big aspect of the problem, of course, me being unemployed and going out with Zoe, the doctor's daughter. I'm sure it's got a lot to do with me not getting anywhere near Bearsden. Can you imagine me sitting in the Bearsden lounge, sipping the Martini, when the old boy strolls in from the golf-course. 'Well, Zoe, so this is the young man who's been entertaining you these last few weeks. Pleased to meet you, my boy. What profession are you hoping to enter yourself?'

I'm not making much of the crossword, so I sink another pint and throw a whisky down after it. Well, there you are. What's green and gets you drunk? Chartreuse? Crème de Menthe? No, a giro. Actually, the drink's beginning to warm me up a bit. That funny feeling from the dream is beginning to die away. I'm getting it straight in my mind what I want to say to Zoe. I'm finally going to tell her straight. I'm not getting aggressive. I don't get aggressive with drink, just philosophical. Things fall into perspective. 'Right, Zoe. What's your game? Let's put our cards on the table. I'm not good enough for your posh pals. Am I right? Admit it. I'm really just another tramp to you, a suitable case for treatment from the soup-kitchen of the heart. A bit of interesting slumming for you? Well, it's no deal, honey. No way. You can't treat this boy like dirt. Pride's my middle name. I've always said it. Take me as you find me or leave me alone. That's the way I live. Always have, always will.

God, it's 8.25! I've never been late for Zoe before!

Well, so what? I drain the last brown, bitter dregs of my Guinness. Let her wait for once. Who the hell does she think she is anyway? I step out of the warm, boozy atmosphere into the grey, pissing rain. It's coming down heavy now. I feel like diving back into the pub, but I turn up my collar and hurry across the road and just about bump into somebody coming round the corner out of Renfield Street. I'm trying to step round him, and Christ! – he's standing there in the rain greeting me. I look up. It figures. It's Dr Kichecky (or Nochecky as he's known). I haven't run into him for months, but whenever you do you can't get past him. He's this old black guy that looks and sounds a bit like Paul Robeson (an old singer my granda used to listen to), but he's a down-and-out who taps you every time he meets you. He goes through the palaver of introducing himself and telling you his cheque hasn't come through and taking your name and address to send what he owes on to you. The story goes that at one time he was a brilliant surgeon till a tragic accident happened. He sewed somebody up with the scalpel still inside them or something and then, through the disgrace, he went down the hill with the drink. It sounds like a Dr Kildare script to me. He has that look of a lifetime loser. Anyway, that's his existence now, padding about the city in an old navy raincoat and his shoes tied round with string and always carrying the same old, cracked, black attaché case.

It's a bit of a joke, bumping into him when I'm on my way to meet Zoe. I shove ten pence into his hand and try to get past him.

But the notebook's out and he's barring my way with, 'Now where shall I send the money when my cheque comes through?'

'Send it to Oxfam!' I shout, and as I turn away I catch a glimpse of his notebook, crammed with pencil-written names and addresses and amounts. And, God above us, there it is, sticking out a mile at the bottom of the grubby page: Zoe's name. I crane round to see it. He snaps the book shut, but it was there definitely: Zoe's name and address and, next to it, 'amount – two pounds'.

'You've done it now!' I whisper at him, menacingly.

'What . . . what do you mean?'

'Zoe! That's what. You're in her power now, one of her debtors. If that cheque doesn't come through at last . . . God help you.'

I walk away from him, laughing out loud, and he stands staring after me as if I'm nuts.

The rain's torrential now. People are scattering off the street into doorways. And there's Zoe, standing in the door of the Odeon waiting for me, her next customer. She's wearing the creamy coat and the mauve shoes with the matching bag, and she's looking at her watch as I square my shoulders and walk up to her. She seems a bit worried, but as soon as she sees me she turns on the smile which, however, falters a bit as I stumble over the kerb.

'Gerry,' she says, knitting her brows and looking at me in that patronizing way, as if I've come out in my true down-and-out colours at last, 'are you drunk?' I'm standing there, swaying slightly, but smiling through the rain and trying to act casual.

'Maybe we'd better go and get you something to eat so you can sober up,' she says, and the Bearsden accent sounds so thick you could cut it with a knife.

'Sober up? What do you mean? I've only had a couple of drinks. Christ! You think I was like that guy in The Happy Moon. Forget it! Let's go in and see the picture.'

'We've missed about twenty minutes of it now,' she says, glancing at her watch.

'Ach well, who cares? They're always slow at the beginning, anyhow. You can pick up the threads as we go along. Come on.'

I take her by the elbow and we step towards the foyer, but she stops. She's looking down, her lips pursed.

'Look, Gerry, I don't think I would enjoy the film now. Perhaps we could see it another night. Why can't we just go for a hamburger or something?'

I step back from her.

'Oh you wouldn't enjoy it, eh? The odour of the alcohol would spoil the pleasure of the Odeon? How awful! Let's go and sort Gerry out first. Stick his head in the horse trough and maybe get him shaved and deloused as well.'

It's all coming out now. All the stuff that was gathering in me in the pub.

Zoe's never heard me speaking like this before. She's looking at me, wide-eyed, and glancing about as if she could do with some help in such strange circumstances.

'That's not very fair, Gerry. After all, you're half an hour late and it's not my fault – '

'Half an hour late! Christ!' I turn my eyes up to the roof and give full vent to the sarcasm. 'Oh how awful! Oh what a big crime! Half an hour late for the hand-out. It's like trying to make your signing on time: "Right, just wait till the queue's through. Now then, explain why you're late. We may have to lapse your payments for this, you know. We have other people to attend to and we can't just run this office to suit you." Come on, Zoe. Get your head out the buttercups. This is the real world!'

'Gerry, what's the matter?' It's an urgent whisper, and there's a pained look in her face. 'Why are you being so aggressive?'

'Aggressive? Who's being aggressive? This is me trying to get you to come clean. Admit the truth. See the facts for what they are. I've let it all wash over me for too long. Well, that's it. I've had a bellyful. I'm putting up with no more indignities!'

It was a good word. I spat it out.

'Indignities? What on earth do you mean, Gerry? What are you talking about?' She's really wide-eyed now and there's a line in the middle of her forehead.

'Oh don't give us that! What do you think I've got, skin or an elephant's hide? I'm not daft, you know. I can see what you're doing. Every time you venture out of Bearsden it's a visit to the slums, an expedition to study the natives. You bring your bag of coloured beads and hand them out if we say something nice. Oh, they're good chaps really, these people, if you know how to treat them right.'

'Gerry, please – '

'Oh don't give me any more of your crap! That's the way you've treated me all along. Just the same as the rest. Just another tramp you're taking an interest in: a donation to Oxfam, a night out with Gerry. Does it all go in the diary at night? Good works done among the lower orders today: pictures with Gerry (required detoxification first); two pounds to Dr Nochecky, an old dilapidated Negro who reminded me of *Uncle Tom's Cabin*.'

'How did you know – '

'Oh we've got a network, you know. The subculture. We're all one big tribe in this city, the lower orders. We report back at night too, pool all the takings, everything we get off the white bwanas.'

I'm in full swing now. Pouring it all out like vomit. Zoe looks stunned.

'Gerry, I don't know how you can say all this,' she says, shaking her head. She sighs and hesitates then, turning up the collar of her coat, she says briskly, 'Anyway, I think I'd better go home now. Goodnight!' and ducks out into the rain.

'It's true. That's how I can say it,' I yell, striding after her. 'It's all been a big freak show to you, hasn't it? Everybody you met when you were with me . . . the old lady, the whole lot. You couldn't wait to make an expedition to the scheme. Never mind if the smell would have made you puke. Your curiosity would have got you there.'

Zoe has stopped. We're facing each other in the pouring rain.

'Oh yes, and what about Gerry all this time? Invite Gerry out to Bearsden? Bloody Bearsden! No way! He might dirty the avenues. Don't take your work home with you. Just visit them in their own patch and observe them. As if we were a bunch of bloody savages!'

And then, I remember, Zoe looks at me as she's never done before.

Her face is white and she's staring hard at me, but saying nothing. It's as if she's seeing me for the first time. I can't think of anything else to say and Zoe just stands there not bothering about the rain.

When she finally speaks, it's almost a whisper.

'How can you be so cruel?' She pauses as if she might get an answer. 'I never invited you out to my house because I felt absolutely certain you wouldn't want to come.' She pauses again, but I still can't think of anything to say. 'If you stop to think of it for one moment, you'll realize that I've never once suggested anywhere we went. Never once. And I've always thought that was the best arrangement. Whatever made you happy was always good enough for me. And any time you've looked unhappy, I've always thought it was me that was doing something wrong, though I've never known what.' It's still the same whisper, but her voice is shaky now. 'As for your mother, I thought she was a delightful person. I would have liked to have met her again. How horrible of you to suggest I was looking down on her! How could you think that? But what's worse is that all this time . . . all the time you've been going out with me, you've had this awful, poisoned idea of me in your head, and you've never said anything about it. It makes me feel so sad, I . . . and all the time, I've been just so pleased to be with you – maybe a bit uneasy sometimes, no wonder, I see now – but really very pleased to be going out with you, and . . . Oh, Gerry, how could you be so cruel and so . . . so unfair?'

Her lip's quivering. 'Wait a minute, Zoe . . .'

'No, I won't wait,' she says, stepping away from me as if she's suddenly discovered I've got rabies. 'I'm going home now and I never want to see you again.'

God! Tears are running down her face!

'Zoe . . .' I move towards her, but she turns and walks away.

She turns back. 'Here! I don't want to keep anything you ever gave me!'

She's opening her bag. Christ! What's coming? I never gave her anything. She throws it at my feet in the rain. It's the folded up picture the Artist did of her. She runs off down into the bright lights and noise of Renfield Street, hunched up, her hands stuck in her coat pockets.

'Zoe! . . . Zoe!' I'm shouting, lurching down the road after her, the Artist's picture clutched in my hand. I collide with somebody running with his head down through the bucketing rain. I stagger on. Zoe's jumping on a bus at the lights – not her bus – any bus to get away from me!

'Zoe! . . . Zoe!' The lights have changed and I'm running full belt as the bus revs away. I'm almost there. I'm reaching for the bar just as the driver shuts the door. I trip and fall into the path of a car gathering speed behind the bus. There's a screech of brakes like a cry of alarm and a scream from the pavement, and I roll over into the gutter as Zoe's bus disappears down the road out of sight.

I'm on my hands and knees watching it. An old couple are shuffling past, arm in arm.

'A young fella the worse for drink, Isa,' comments the old guy without looking at me.

I limp away back up through the sodden city and end up in a corner in some nondescript, old man's boozer, I don't know where, drinking the last of my week's money.

The next morning hit me on the head like a ton of cold water. My guts contracted every time an image from the night before came to the surface. I stuck my head in the pan and put my fingers down my throat and spewed. It must have been a bad pint, I told the old lady. 'Well, you will drink,' she says.

If this was one of those *True Romance* stories or something out of the *Jackie*, I would tell you how the truth about Zoe now emerged like suppressed evidence after a rigged trial. It would all come out with a rush: how Zoe had never been out with a boy before me; how her father was a drunkard who used to batter Zoe and her mother; how he's now offsky down to England, leaving their lives in ruins after they've been virtual prisoners in the Bearsden bungalow for years; how Zoe rebuilds their lives, tending the mother, who's now a physical and mental wreck, with constant loving care; how they've got hardly a penny to live on; how Zoe meets a boy she thinks is wonderful because he takes her to restaurants and gets her portrait done and so on; how I realize I've thrown away a pearl, but it's too late now, or is it?

As you'll know, life's never really like that, but, as the days went by it came home to me that what I actually knew about Zoe you could have written on the back of a stamp. And then one day when I met Dunky and the girlfriend and I started hearing things about Zoe that sounded as if they might just have a vague resemblance to that *True Romance* story, I made an excuse and hurried away, shuddering, in case the whole thing would come true.

There were many phone calls to Zoe, but she didn't want to know. Her old lady answered in a clipped tone: Zoe was not available. Or the phone was put down as soon as I spoke. She couldn't even bear to speak to me. I was unforgiveable. I even wrote, but she didn't reply. It was dead, the whole thing. I've never seen Zoe since.

So here I am, a year later, back in The South Pacific hoping for what, I don't know. The Artist is plying his trade with a baldy, middle-aged guy who looks like a shabby office clerk out for his lunch-break. He's forking chips into his mouth and reading his paper, while the Artist sketches.

'Now, what colour are your eyes, sir?'

'Bloodshot.'

A moment's nervous hesitation of the Artist's fingers over the pencil pocket. 'Oh, don't say that,' he says, pulling out the blue and finishing the sketch.

'That's nothing like me,' says the clerk, glancing up from his

Daily Express. 'It's more like Humpty Dumpty with a moustache, for God's sake.'

'Well, that's the way the Artist sees you.'

'Here! Scram!' The clerk pushes fifty pence across the table. The Artist tips his hat and departs with his money.

The drawing falls over the edge of the table and floats down on to the floor. The old clerk goes back to his dinner and his paper.

SHARON, THE FERRYMAN'S DAUGHTER
Valerie Thornton

That she should live on an island in the middle of the river was more than appropriate. Her father was the ferryman. If you wanted to cross the river, you hung a white-painted board on a pair of hooks at the end of the rudimentary pier, then when Sharon's father noticed this, he set out for you in his small boat following a graceful upstream curve to counter the current.

Every morning he rowed his daughter to the shore. But she didn't join the cheerful mob who came to school in the low blue single-decker. Nor did she walk with friends in a chattering swirl of blue uniforms.

Sharon walked alone, by the most direct route, up over the top of the town, past Battlefield Street with the cannons in the middle of it and down along the edge of the George Park towards the school. She would stand alone, her stout walking shoes and thick socks setting her apart from the rest, waiting for the bell.

For all the walking she did, she invariably looked under the weather. She had a long pasty face with a suggestion of spots. Her eyes were pale blue with pale blue National Health glasses, her teeth were long and dirty, and her long hair, which was an unpleasant peachy shade, was greasy and lank as far down as her shoulders.

No one wanted her as their friend. Apart from being inaccessible after school, she had also come late to the school, joining in third year, and her mother was dead. Everyone had established their exclusive cliques and as Sharon wasn't beautiful, they greeted her with studied indifference.

She wasn't victimized as could easily have happened. Just left alone. If you did speak to her, she replied with a whining, nasal voice, speaking softly. She didn't hide behind an assumed dignity, nor was she obviously upset at her situation. She simply accepted her insular position while life flowed around her.

Someone must have been talking to her though, because as soon as it was known that she had found a boyfriend, she became the centre of attention. Her boyfriend was no mere pupil, not even a fifth or sixth year boy for whom many a third year girl longed, but a man. She maintained he was twenty-three. No one was quite sure if it was true or not, so she was cross-questioned in the toilets until everyone was satisfied that she wasn't making it all up.

'And how did you meet him?'

'Walking home from school one day. He asked where I was going, and if he could come with me.'

'What's his name?'

'John.'

'John what?'

'I don't know,' she giggled a little. 'I haven't asked him yet . . .'

'And what do you do?'

'We go down by the river and walk and hold hands and sometimes we kiss.'

'What's it like?'

She thinks a little, then shrugs her shoulders.

'It's OK. Sometimes he lets me have a puff at his cigarette, but I don't like it very much.'

'Does your Dad know?'

'No, not yet.'

'Are you going to tell him?'

'I don't think so.'

She flashes an uncertain smile with her long yellow teeth. You wonder what sort of man would go with her.

One day she announces they are going to the pictures. Saturday afternoon, so her father won't suspect. No one is sure whether to believe her or not. Afterwards they test her with questions about the cinema, and one girl who's seen the film asks her about the plot.

'I don't remember that bit. We were kissing a lot. One kiss lasted for fifteen whole minutes!'

This was unheard of. She was asked in detail about it.

'Well, he put his hand along the back of the seat, then round here.'

She touches her breast pocket. Those who know about these things nod approvingly.

'Then he sort of pulled me and started kissing me, and just kept on.' She lowers her voice. 'His tongue was there too. But I didn't like that bit very much. It was all slippy.'

The wise ones nod in agreement. She certainly didn't seem to be making it all up. But they wanted proof.

'Why don't you get him to meet you at school? Is he good-looking?'

'I don't know,' she giggles. 'I mean, I could ask him and see what he says . . . I don't know if you'd think he was good-looking. He's got nice blue eyes and dark brown hair. We just always meet down by the river . . . '

'Are you going to the pictures again?'

'I don't think so. I'm scared my Dad'll find out. He'd probably kill me.'

One day she says he's going to meet her in the park, after school.

'Go and sit on one of the benches with him so that we can walk past and have a good look at him.'

'I'll try.'

All through the afternoon classes there's an expectant air. The girls in the row by the window look down into the park trying to spot the boyfriend. At four, everyone dithers over their packing up in order to let Sharon out first.

They form small curious groups and several who would have gone for the bus at the school gates decide to walk through the park.

Sharon is sitting on the roundabout, holding hands with a man. She is bursting with pride and self-consciousness. They sweep round in slow circles, displaying themselves to not only Sharon's classmates but to all the other pupils above and below them who also pass homewards through the park.

John seems a bit uncomfortable about being on display. He is unshaven and unkempt. His greasy black hair is lank, in sympathy with Sharon's greasy hair which is the colour of those discoloured tufts around the mouths of white dogs. He wears a dirty blue anorak which fails to conceal a fair-sized beer belly, and he looks old and surly. Nonetheless he's there, with her, and obviously her boyfriend. He decides to leave and tugs her off the roundabout. He takes her away, his arm heavily around her shoulder, her head tilted against his shoulder, awkwardly.

The next day in the toilets everyone is a little reserved. Her pride embarrasses them.

'He's really nice, Sharon!' they gush, and she beams.

'You really look as if you're in love!'

'We are!' she says, her eyes bright. At times she can look almost pretty – if she washed her hair and tried a little eyeshadow.

'He gave me something last night, after school.'

'What?' they chorus with unconcealed curiosity.

'Look!'

She loosens her tie and drags her shirt back from the side of her neck. A livid, bite-shaped bruise nestles there.

'Can you see it? Is it still there?'

No one knows what to say.

'Does it hurt?' someone asks.

'A little, but it's quite a nice kind of hurt.'

She fingers it briefly, then covers it up and tightens her tie.

'It's a love bite. It's the first love bite I've ever had!' she says proudly. 'He says he'll give me some more too.'

Sharon is a celebrity.

One day she tells them John has given her love bites all the way down her front. No one is sure whether to believe her or not. Only a few around her throat are visible in PE and she won't reveal the rest.

That afternoon she is called out of class to go and see the headmistress. She can't be in trouble. She's one of the quietest, most biddable pupils in the class.

She comes back much later, her eyes rimmed red, and sniffing. The teacher makes no comment. At the interval they cluster around her in the toilet while she cries openly.

'I don't know what to do,' she rocks herself in misery. No one touches her.

'What happened?'

'She asked to see . . . I had to undo my blouse, and she saw them all.' 'Was she angry?'

'No, not really. She asked if my Dad knew.'

'And he doesn't?'

'No. She said if I didn't stop seeing him she'd tell my Dad.'

'But how does she know?'

'She asked me all about him. I had to tell her,' a sob racked her. 'I don't want to stop seeing John – I love him! She says I'm too young for him, but I'm not! He loves me too, I know, he told me, last night, when he gave me these,' she pressed her hand to her chest. 'I even had a note to get me off swimming, but I forgot it was PE.'

'Did you tell her you would stop seeing him?'

'I had to. But I won't. We'll just have to keep it a secret.'

'When are you seeing him again?'

'Today, after school. Down by the river. He says he's not coming back to the park again,' she laughed a little. 'You've all scared him off.'

'What are you going to tell him?'

'I don't know.'

Sharon was subdued and withdrawn the next day.

'Well, did you see him?'

'Did you tell him?'

'What did he say?'

She smiled quietly and hugged herself.

'He was really nice about it. We went to a place he knew, a sort of hut at the bottom of the fields, and talked about it for ages. He just said it didn't make any difference to us and that he loved me. And he gave me something too, to prove it.'

She hesitates, considering what to say.

'What? More love bites? Where?'

Her demeanour becomes almost withering.

'No, much better.'

'What then?'

A note of hesitancy creeps into the interrogators. A gulf of ignorance is opening between them. Sharon is suddenly wise.

'This!' she decides, holding out her hand. A little silver ring, heart-shaped, is on her middle finger. 'I have to take it off when I go home, but I put it on in bed.'

'It's lovely!' they breathe. But Sharon is beyond them now. Beyond asking. Beyond telling.

The next day she is pale and worried. John wasn't there last night.

'Maybe he's not well. Do you know where he stays?'

'No.'

Nor was he there that evening.

Nor the next.

Sharon would sit in class and twist her ring endlessly while the others retreated from her. She began to be off school, ill, sick. Instead of getting over John she became increasingly morose and would hold herself alone, pale and silent.

Then she stopped coming to school altogether.

Some said her father had found out and wouldn't let her out of his sight. Others said she'd eloped with John. Someone said she'd thrown herself in the river and that her body still hadn't been found. And one girl, much later on, said she'd seen a girl who looked a bit like Sharon pushing a pram.

But that was much later on and by then most of them had forgotten about her.

THE NEW BOY
Geddes Thomson

Tam was in a good mood that morning. His mum had had a big win at the bingo the night before. She had brought home some special fish suppers, two bottles of Irn Bru and a big red box of chocolates. A nice surprise on a Tuesday night, with the rain running down the windows, no money for the gas fire and the telly rotten as usual.

She had given Tam five one pound notes which now nestled in his jerkin pocket. It was a great feeling, pound notes in your pocket. He would pass the day thinking about what he would do with all that money. Better than listening to moany old teachers.

He was explaining all this to his mate, Alec, as they dragged their feet through the school gate, when he first saw the new boy.

Tam nudged Alec. 'Whose zat?'

'Doan know. Never seen im before.'

The new boy was surrounded by a crowd of first years. He was a big broad-shouldered lad with a sun-tanned face and dark curly hair. He was dressed in a fancy pullover and brown corduroys and he was wearing a tie. The first years seemed to be enjoying his company, because they were laughing and skipping about him like a pack of playful dogs.

Tam stopped and stared at the newcomer in *his* playground. He didn't like the way the first years were listening to the new boy's every word. Tam was used to younger boys looking up to *him* as a kind of leader.

'Hullo,' shouted the new boy.

'Talking tae me, son, or chewin a brick?' Tam shouted back.

The first years stopped their capering and edged away like cowboys in a western when the goodie and the baddie meet up in the saloon. The new boy was suddenly alone which didn't seem to bother him one little bit.

'Braw mornin,' he said.

'*Braw Morning!*' Tam imitated. 'Who the hell ur you? Oor

61

Wullie or somethin? Listen. We rule here, pal. Don't forget it. OK?'

Just then the bell went. The playground began to empty. Tam turned away and swaggered towards the technical block. He felt the crinkly pound notes in his pocket.

Tam didn't see the new boy again till the second last period of the morning – English. It was one of his better subjects. Mr Campbell wasn't as moany as the other teachers and there wasn't anything special to learn in English.

'Seasy,' he told Alec. 'Ah kin speak it, can't ah? No like that bloody French. Ivrybody should talk English. Wan languidge fur ivrybody.'

Alec decided there must be something wrong with that argument. 'Yiv goat tae huv different languidges. It's their culture n'at. How are aw the foreigners gonny learn English?'

Tam didn't answer because a snobby girl prefect with gold braid on her blazer had just brought in the new boy.

'See whit the cat's dragged in,' he whispered to Alec. 'Big heid the breid.'

The new boy was nearly as tall as Mr Campbell. He looked perfectly relaxed and smiled broadly, not the slight shy smile of an ordinary new pupil. Mr Campbell directed him to a seat at the back of the room beside Kathy Milligan.

They were doing a project about advertising. It was called 'The Hidden Persuaders'. Mr Campbell always had fancy titles like that for his English projects. But Tam quite liked him and usually he weighed in with a few answers just to keep him happy.

Today Mr Campbell was on about TV adverts, asking the class for their favourites. Tam, aware of the new boy somewhere behind him, put up his hand.

'Ah like the one about biscuits, Sir.'

Mr Campbell smiled encouragingly.

'Tell us about it, Tom.'

'Well it's these Mexican bandits an they rob a bank an the federales come an it's fur this biscuit.'

'I know the one you mean. Why do you like it?'

Tam decided to show off, show the new boy how gallus he was.

'Well, ah like the burds, Sir. Lovely burds in that ad.'

Alec spluttered with laughter, but Mr Campbell was not so easily put off. '*Why* do they have – young ladies – in the advert?' There was a pause. 'Yes, Colin?'

Tam heard the voice of the new boy behind him. 'It's tae mak ye think the product is . . . glamorous. Tae . . . tae connect it wae nice ideas so that ye'll gae oot an buy it.'

Everybody turned round to look. They realized that he had put into words what had been vaguely going through their own minds.

Mr Campbell was delighted. 'That's a very good answer, Colin. A *very* good answer.'

But Colin wasn't finished yet. 'Tak this lassie aside me, Sir. Now if she was tae recommend biscuits oan the TV, I wid definitely buy them because she looks sae nice.'

Tam narrowed his eyes and glared. Kathy Milligan's dark head was lowered, but he could see her blush and smile. He had quite fancied Kathy Milligan for a long time and here was this character giving her the patter already.

Tam was never sure how to deal with girls. Once, in the corridor, he had smiled at Kathy Milligan and punched her on the arm.

'Why did you do that?' Alec had asked.

'Ah – like er.'

'You *like* er!' Alec had laughed. 'Ye've goat a funny way a showin it. What would ye do if ye *didny* like er? Break er arm?'

Alec was nudging him. 'This guy's quite a character, Tam!'

Tam stared at Alec and chose his words carefully. 'This guy,' he said, 'is a *snob* an a *swot* and ah'm gonny sort him out.'

'He's big.'

'Aye, a big drip. Wears a tie, talks funny, gies good answers. He's a big,' Tam stopped, searching for the word that would sum up what he felt about the new boy. 'He's a big tube.'

'Kathy Milligan likes im.'

Tam suddenly realized that his so-called pal, Alec, was deliberately annoying him and didn't answer.

For the rest of the period he day-dreamed about how he would sort out the new boy.

The last period of the morning was PE. Once again the new boy was in his class. Tam watched him closely in the dressing-room and nudged Alec when the new boy took a pair of shining white shorts out of his duffle bag.

'Look whit snobby's goat.'

Tam wore his own black shorts under his jeans. He never carried anything to school, even a pencil. If you tried to carry things around they just got lost. And then there was trouble.

'Ah still think e's big.' It was Alec again. Sometimes Tam wondered why he bothered with Alec, because Alec wasn't normal. He supported Partick Thistle for a start. Partick Thistle!

Tam decided to needle his friend. 'See me an him. It'll be like Rangers and Partick Thistle. Nae contest. The bigger they are, the harder they faw.'

The PE teacher, Mr Simpson, appeared, bouncing a football on the stone floor. Big Sim he was called and he was as hard as nails. That was why Tam never forgot his shorts.

'OK,' Big Sim said. 'Pay attention, lads. Football in the top playground and nothing above head height because of the windows. Got that?'

Big Sim's cold blue eyes flicked over them, one by one, looking for any boy without his full kit, but even wee Sammy, who didn't know the day of the week, had brought his gear.

Out in the playground they were divided into teams. Tam was pleased to see that he was in the opposite team from the new boy. Now he would show him who was the boss.

The game started. The orange football began to skid around the playground chased by the players.

After a few minutes the new boy, who turned out to be a good player, dribbled towards Tam. As he went past Tam tripped him, making it look like an accidental late tackle. The new boy fell his full length on the concrete playground. His nose was in a puddle and his knee was bleeding. The white shorts were splattered with mud.

Big Sim came pounding up, blowing his whistle and waving his arms like a big-time referee as the boys crowded round the figure on the ground.

'Get back, you lot. Are you OK lad? Any damage?'

The new boy smiled. 'Ah'm fine, Sir. Ah've just skint ma knee. That's aw. Accidents happen, ye ken.'

But Tam sensed that the rest of them didn't think it was an accident. He heard Alec's whisper over his left shoulder: 'See you. You're mental!'

For the rest of the game he hardly got a kick at the ball, but the new boy's name began to ring out over the playground.

'Well done, Colin.'

'Nice pass, Colin.'

'Great goal, Colin.'

Afterwards, in the dressing-room, Tam pulled on his clothes without a word to anybody. He felt that somehow he had suffered a great defeat and he wasn't quite sure how it had happened. OK, he had tripped the guy. So what? That was nothing.

Five minutes later Tam sat in the shelter and watched the entrance of the PE building. He felt a tension that tightened his throat and neck so that he could hardly breathe.

At last he saw the new boy come out the glass doors and look around as if searching for something. Or someone.

Tam rose to his feet in the dark shelter. Slowly he walked out into the sunlight. The new boy saw him. He was waving something in his hand.

'Can ah see ye a meenit?' he shouted in that funny accent which grated on Tam's nerves.

'Ah suppose you can,' Tam shouted back, 'unless you're blind.'

The new boy was now standing in front of him. Alec was right. He *was* big. Tam had to look up into the broad brown face.

'The bigger they are the harder they faw.' That was what he had told Alec. It had been a favourite saying of his father's. 'The bigger they are the harder they faw.'

Tam clenched his fists inside his jerkin pockets.

'Something wrang?' the new boy asked.

'Aye,' Tam said. '*You*'re wrang. You've been wrang since the minute ah saw ye. Who *are* you? Where do you come fae?'

The new boy opened his mouth to answer and, at that moment, Tam jumped him in a flurry of swirling arms and thudding fists. He heard the new boy gasp in pain, but he also felt knuckles crash into his own face. Desperately, he grabbed his enemy round the waist and the two of them swayed and tottered round the playground like two drunk men until they crashed to the ground.

Tam had him locked round the waist in a vice-like grip, but the new boy had an equally strong hold on Tam's neck.

After a minute like this he heard Colin MacDonald say, 'You let me go and ah'll let *you* go.'

Tam strengthened his grip while he thought about this. It might be a trick. On the other hand, Tam could feel his strength slowly draining away. He decided he had better take the offer while there was still time.

'One – two – three!' And Tam let go and at the same moment felt the arms drop away from his own neck.

They lay side by side on the hard playground. Exhausted.

'Yer a bonny fighter,' he heard the new boy say.

'Yer no sae bad, yersel,' Tam had to admit.

'Oh an ah've goat something fur ye,' Colin MacDonald sat up and opened his big brown fist to reveal a heap of green paper. 'Ah fund them in the dressing-room. They're yours, aren't they? Ah wis comin tae gie them tae yi.'

The pound notes. No longer new and crinkly, but crushed and dirty.

They grinned at each other.

THE STAR
Alasdair Gray

A star had fallen beyond the horizon, in Canada perhaps. (He had an aunt in Canada.) The second was nearer, just beyond the iron works, so he was not surprised when the third fell into the backyard. A flash of gold light lit the walls of the enclosing tenements and he heard a low musical chord. The light turned deep red and went out, and he knew that somewhere below a star was cooling in the night air. Turning from the window he saw that no one else had noticed. At the table his father, thoughtfully frowning, filled in a football coupon, his mother continued ironing under the pulley with its row of underwear. He said in a small voice, 'A'm gawn out.' His mother said, 'See you're no' long then.' He slipped through the lobby and on to the stairhead, banging the door after him.

The stairs were cold and coldly lit at each landing by a weak electric bulb. He hurried down three flights to the black silent yard and began hunting backward and forward, combing with his fingers the lank grass round the base of the clothes-pole. He found it in the midden on a decayed cabbage leaf. It was smooth and round, the size of a glass marble, and it shone with a light which made it seem to rest on a precious bit of green and yellow velvet. He picked it up. It was warm and filled his cupped palm with a ruby glow. He put it in his pocket and went back upstairs.

That night in bed he had a closer look. He slept with his brother who was not easily wakened. Wriggling carefully far down under the sheets, he opened his palm and gazed. The star shone white and blue, making the space around him like a cave in an iceberg. He brought it close to his eye. In its depth was the pattern of a snowflake, the grandest thing he had ever seen. He looked through the flake's crystal lattice into an ocean of glittering blue-black waves under a sky full of huge galaxies. He heard a remote lulling sound like the sound in a sea shell, and fell asleep with the star safely clenched in his hand.

He enjoyed it for nearly two weeks, gazing at it each night

below the sheets, sometimes seeing the snowflake, sometimes a flower, jewel, moon or landscape. At first he kept it hidden during the day but soon took to carrying it about with him; the smooth rounded gentle warmth in his pocket gave comfort when he felt insulted or neglected.

At school one afternoon he decided to take a quick look. He was at the back of the classroom in a desk by himself. The teacher was among the boys at the front row and all heads were bowed over books. Quickly he brought out the star and looked. It contained an aloof eye with a cool green pupil which dimmed and trembled as if seen through water.

'What have you there, Cameron?'

He shuddered and shut his hand.

'Marbles are for the playground, not the classroom. You'd better give it to me.'

'I cannae, sir.'

'I don't tolerate disobedience, Cameron. Give me that thing.'

The boy saw the teacher's face above him, the mouth opening and shutting under a clipped moustache. Suddenly he knew what to do and put the star in his mouth and swallowed. As the warmth sank toward his heart he felt relaxed and at ease. The teacher's face moved into the distance. Teacher, classroom, world receded like a rocket into a warm, easy blackness leaving behind a trail of glorious stars, and he was one of them.

BARELY AN INCIDENT
Dilys Rose

She ran into the station just in time to see the tail-lights of her train being sucked away into the dark throat of the tunnel. Above the shuttle platform, blue banners swayed in its wake, like drunks. More time to be put to no good use.

The station was deserted and freezing, as only a station could be, icy draughts snaking in from all corners. Snow had fallen earlier, turning to sleet and finally rain. Wet dripped through holes in the roof, where neurotic city birds were twittering away, duped by round-the-clock lighting into believing it was day and time to sing. The lino-tiled concourse was slittered with coffee, beer and slush. In the far corner, a hunched woman was pushing a brush, eyeing the floor with contempt, as if there were no point in doing what would just have to be done all over again.

The station was bleak at the best of times and if you couldn't face the bar and its odour of weary, anonymous transience, there was nowhere to sit, except the dank Superloos or the slippery metal seating-rings, stuck out on the concourse like high-tech doughnuts. Whoever designed those seats must have been convinced that the last thing a traveller wants is to be friendly. Folk fanned away from each other, like spokes on a wheel, points on a compass. A deliberate effort was required to catch your neighbour's eye.

It was too cold, exposed and lonely out on the doughnut seats so she stood in the entrance to the carry-out burger bar, where an overhead heater puffed out stingy clouds of warmth. She should eat, but one look at the blown-up photos of buns oozing melted cheese and sweaty beef and she was digging in her pockets for cigarettes. The news-stand, coffee bar and fruitbarrow were closed and barred for the night. If you really needed to spend money, you could still get passport photos from the curtained booth, business cards from the autoprinter, donate to city hospitals by dropping money into a Howitzer shell, or Test Your Emotional Temperature on The Passion Chart, if you were prepared to squeeze a couple of phallic handlebars. Nothing else to do but look at the clock, the Arrivals and Departures board – on which nothing was imminent – and the people.

Apart from a bag lady who was curled round one of the ring seats like a seal, asleep – or trying to be – the only people using the seats were a young couple, Japanese perhaps, or Malaysian, she couldn't tell, couldn't really see them clearly because three lads, lager cans in hand, had rocked to a halt in front of them, stamping their boots and splashing filth from the floor at the small, compact couple and their tidy bundle of belongings.

– Sorry, mate, one of them said, Ah mean ah'm really f— sorry but.

He squinted at his can – it had a pin-up on the back – took a swig, tipped it so the dregs dribbled on to the girl's shoes, staggered back a couple of steps, steadied himself briefly, then reeled in the direction of the taxi rank. The other two were still standing over the pair on the seat. One of them bent down so his eyes were on a level with the boy, and inches away from his face.

– Heh heh – WHO FLUNG DUNG?

There was a flurry of movement on the seat, a flash of white shirt as the boy twisted to get a better grip of his girlfriend, jerking her towards him. With his free hand he pushed a blue-black lick of hair out of his eyes. His eyes batted from side to side as if they were on elastic.

– Ah said, WHO FLUNG DUNG?

– Don't know, said the boy. Sorry. Don't know. His panicky vowels rolled around the empty station like skittles.

– That's a good one, eh, Barry? Bastard disnae know.

– Does he no?

– No. Nothing like ignorance, eh?

– You put him right, man, put him in the picture.

– Ach, wouldnae waste ma breath.

The girl began to cry, quietly. She had her glasses off and was plugging up the tears with her fingertips but the shiny drops kept oozing through, breaking up and trailing down her cheeks like scars or wrinkles. The boy circled her with his arms, putting his body in front of hers like a shield or a blanket, as if by enveloping her he could mend the damage, make the tears stop. He was talking non-stop into her chest, rocking the girl against him.

– Ah'm starvin, man, so ah am.

– Fancy a chinky, eh? Deid cat chop suey. Hey – WHO FLUNG DUNG!

The automatic doors wheezed open and shut the three of them out, leaving behind the sour echo of their laughter. And just as they left, in walked a couple of the boys in blue. It was farcical – the timing was spot-on – but not funny. They were doing the rounds, a gangly one and an older, stockier one, strolling, chatting amiably. They were not looking around much, just glancing here and there, as if they didn't want to notice anything they might have to deal with, as if they were actually trying not to pay attention.

Should she report the incident, get the bastards booked? Names, addresses, questions, notes in the wee black book. It was provocation, no doubt about it. But it could have been worse, what might have happened could have been so much worse. No blood, wounds, no visible damage, nothing you could put a finger on, barely an incident and yet anger welled up in her – anger and hate. She wanted revenge, reprisals, wanted them dragged back and paraded through the square, chained at the neck, their tongues cut out and all the other atrocities race had committed on race. But mostly she wanted the girl to stop crying.

It was terrible, seeing the boy trying so hard to comfort the girl and getting nowhere, the pair of them a contorted huddle of distress, shipwrecked on the concourse. The boys in blue ignored them. The gangly one jerked a thumb at the bag lady humping about under her coat. The stocky one checked his watch and shrugged. They'd shift her later.

She was standing right where they had stood, in a puddle of spilt lager.

– Excuse me.

–

– Excuse me but were those people bothering you?

– Don't know, don't know!

The boy sprang up from the seat, fist raised, eyes flashing. She jumped back, expecting a blow, but the boy checked himself in mid-swing. The girl stared, open-mouthed and impassive. Up close she could see how young they were. Pimply kids in thin clothes. First loves maybe. Wanting to draw a curtain on the world. But the world wouldn't be shut out, go away or mind its own business.

– Those people . . .

She pointed in the direction of the automatic doors. She hadn't even thought of what to say, just walked right up, intruded, forced herself on them.

– They're just drunk. Don't pay any attention. Please.

But that wasn't it. That wasn't what she'd meant to say at all, and she could hear the plaintive whine in her voice. The boy lowered his arm slowly, sat down and resumed his grip on the girl. She fiddled with her glasses, clicking the legs against the frames, lifting them to her eyes then, changing her mind, slamming them into her lap. What's it to you, her eyes demanded, What's it to you?

– You are very kind thank you for your trouble.

The boy's words rattled out, a memorized response, polite standby for any occasion.

– It's no trouble, she said, To me. It's you who had the trouble. Sorry, she said. I'm really sorry.

There was nothing more to say and she was getting uncomfortable and embarrassed by the whole thing. There was no sign of her train yet, so she walked back to her spot outside the burger bar and went on waiting, making a point of not looking in the direction of the seats. She was tired, of people, herself, of hate and stupidity, wasted time and missed connections, the weight of work in her bag, tired of being out.

Maybe the girl had been upset about something else, maybe they hadn't even understood the insult, maybe the two of them had been fighting, or somebody they knew was sick, or recently deceased. Maybe she'd failed an exam – they looked more like students than tourists – or lost her job, or even just been to see a film with a sad ending. What did she know? The girl could have been crying about all kinds of things.

As she hurried across the concourse towards the train pulling up on platform six, she glanced back. The girl was still crying.

Her blundering spiel had done nothing to help. Maybe even made things worse. After all, when did anybody ever thank you for poking your nose in, interfering. And what she'd said – *those people* – what did she really know about them? And *just drunk*. Just? What kind of excuse was that? – Sorry, I don't know, don't remember, am not in control of what I'm doing because I've had too much to drink – The national excuse for everything, from bad-mouthing to murder. And she had gone along with it, just like everybody else.

Saturday Song
Maureen Monaghan

He was about fourteen, clean, tidy and unlovely. Some sort of skin complaint, he was told; you'll grow out of it soon, he was promised. Meanwhile, he kept his boiled-looking face as much to himself as possible, and when he rubbed and scratched the raw cracks in his hands under his school desk, the teacher asked him what he was fidgeting with, and the other boys sniggered. Apart from scratching his hands, he seldom made any superfluous movements. So he was not kicking stones or crushing handfuls of the dusty hedge on that bright October morning. He just sat quietly on a low wall, clutching a small case and a cheap plastic folder under his arm. The wall faced the back of a row of crumbling houses, and the boy was staring absently at a broken window in the second house from the end.

An old man came slowly along the lane and into the yard. When he saw the boy, he stiffened, straightened his back and gathered his bulging string shopping bags close to him.

'What do you want?' He sounded weary. There was no answer. 'I said, what d'you want?' There was fear in the old man's voice.

There was a pause, then the boy said, 'Nothing. I'm just waiting.'

'Well you can't wait here. On your way, laddie!'

'No. I'll just stay. It's too early to go yet. I won't get in your way.' The boy spoke politely.

The old man almost mustered a roar, 'Move, son! I suppose it was your lot done that! Just get out of here and leave me in peace. Away home and break your own windows!'

'I'm sorry about your window,' said the boy, 'but I've just got here.' He stood up. 'I'm only waiting for a while, but I'll move along there if you like.'

He turned towards the old man, towards the other end of the shabby terrace, his mild blue eyes blinking and watering in the sun. There was no menace in him after all, no anger, except in the red blotchy skin. The old man sagged, too tired to argue any more. He handed over his bags and his keys as if to a neighbour of long standing. 'Will you carry the messages in for me, lad? They're heavier than I thought.'

The door opened into a narrow, stone-floored hallway smelly with paraffin cans, old newspapers and the passing attentions of cats. The boy had to squeeze himself against flaking, grey distemper to let the old man pass him and open the door half-way along the hall. A new set of smells and the twittering of a budgie greeted them as they entered the living-room.

The boy almost retched as the combined odours of birdcage, bed and old age reached him. The old man, unnoticing, said, 'Come in, son. This is where I live. It's not very grand, but it does me fine. Could you put some coal on? It's a bit cold.'

He sank into a worn, lumpy armchair. The boy put the string bags on the table and laid down his own case and folder too. He looked around for tongs or a shovel, then used his hands, reluctantly.

'Who's C.P.M.?'

The boy turned, startled. The old man was looking at the case. 'Oh, that was my Dad, Colin Peter Morrison. I'm just Peter.'

'Your Dad's passed on, then? What's in the case?'

'Nothing. A clarinet. It was my Dad's.'

The old man looked eager. 'Can you play it?'

'No!'

'Not even a wee bit?'

'No. I hate it!'

'Are you learning to play it?'

'No. My Mum sent me to lessons. But I hate it. Can I wash my hands?'

'Over there. Why d'you hate it?'

But Peter turned on the tap and washed his hands carefully. Then since the water was hot, he wiped out the greasy sink and started to wash the dishes which were in the sink, beside the sink, on the table and on the mantelpiece. He wet an old cloth which was bundled on the wooden draining-board, and washed off the ash and coal-dust and tea stains from the hearth. He looked at the filthy cloth.

'I think I should just throw this away now.'

'Aye! You're a tidy fellow. D'you like the bird? Her name's Jinty. She's good company.'

'Uh-huh. My Dad used to keep birds, but my Mum never liked them. I could clean out the cage. Does she get out?'

'She'll not go far. She likes the mantelpiece.'

Peter opened the cage door with the bird trying to peck his fingers. It fluttered on to the old man's head, flew over to one of the square, varnished bedposts and finally settled on the brightly painted toffee-tin above the fireplace, squawking quietly.

The old man said soothingly, 'Sssh, beauty, sssh! He's just making your house nice. He'll not hurt you.'

Peter crossed to the sink to fill the little water bowl. 'Where d'you keep the birdseed?'

'Here, I've just bought some more. She'll soon get used to you.' He hesitated, then added, 'She'll know you next time.'

'Mr Briggs, could I . . . ?'

'How d'you know my name?' the old man asked sharply.

'Your pension book. It's on the mantelpiece. It's just a different colour from my Mum's.'

'Don't miss much, do you, son?' he mumbled.

'Mr Briggs, I could come for a while on Saturdays, and . . . and help you. You know, clean up a bit, or go to the shops. I haven't . . . I mean, there's nothing else to do.' Peter held his finger out to the budgie. The bird ignored him, flew back to the cage and warbled at its reflection in the tiny mirror. 'Would you like me to wash the window? I've still got time.'

'Leave it, lad. You can do it next week.'

Peter shut the door of the birdcage. 'Oh! Fine! I'll come about ten.'

'That'll be nice.' The old man's gaze was resting on the clarinet case. 'Why d'you hate it?'

'What? Oh! I just do.'

'Play us a tune.'

'No! I've told you! I can't. I'll need to go now.' The red patches glowed on Peter's face and neck.

'What were you waiting for, son?'

'Nothing. It doesn't matter.' Behind his back he rubbed his

itching hands against his trousers, against each other. 'Will I come next Saturday then?'

He tucked the clarinet and the folder under his arm. The old man was running his thumb-nail back and forward over the top of the birdcage. 'What d'you think, Jinty? Will we let him come back? Maybe he'll give us a tune next time.'

The bird cocked its head, first to one side, then to the other. Peter opened the door into the damp hallway.

'Jinty says you can come. You could wait at the end of the lane and carry the messages. If you want to.'

Peter's fiery skin began to cool. 'Right! Cheerio! See you on Saturday, Mr Briggs.'

'Shut the doors behind you, son!'

Peter shut the living-room door. Going down the hall, he added shyly, 'Cheerio, Jinty.'

Their Saturday mornings settled into an easy routine. Peter, always with the clarinet and music-folder under his arm, would meet Mr Briggs outside the corner shop. The old man would hand over his bags and they would walk slowly, companionably, along the lane which became barer and muddier as the weeks went on. Once inside the house, the boy would fill the coal buckets while the old man made tea. They would drink it in front of the fire and slip cake crumbs to the budgie through the bars of the cage. Then Peter would gather up everything that looked like rubbish, take it out to the dustbin and push an ancient, rattling sweeper over the thin carpet. He would clean out the birdcage, and wash the window, if it wasn't raining. Mr Briggs would potter around, put away his meagre groceries, start to peel potatoes, then abandon them in favour of another mug of stewed tea.

The conversation was hardly more varied than the housework.

'And how's the school, lad?'

'Fine.'

'Doing all right then?'

'Uh-huh.'

'You mind and stick in. I wish I had.'

'Uh-huh.'

Peter would brace himself for the next bit.

'How about a wee tune, then? Me and Jinty would like a wee tune. Wouldn't we, beauty?' The bird would trill obligingly.

Sometimes the old man held out the clarinet case towards the boy. Sometimes he would open it and stroke the red plush lining, or run his finger along the dark, shiny wood. 'C'mon son. Play us a tune.'

'No! I can't.'

'Aw, you could if you tried.'

'I don't want to!'

Mr Briggs would shake his head, sigh loudly and return to his potato peeling, looking hurt. Eventually he would say, 'Is there time for more tea?'

And Peter would look at his watch, pick up his things and say, 'No. I'd better be going. Will I come again next week?'

They would both look round the hot, tidy room.

'Aye, laddie. See you next Saturday.'

The last Saturday in November was wild and stormy. Peter was already soaked by the time Mr Briggs came out of the shop with his usual string bags tucked inside plastic carriers. They ploughed along the filthy lane, heads down against the rain, bumping into each other as they fought the wind. The old man kept tugging at his hat and pulling up his coat collar, but Peter had the shopping in one hand and the clarinet and music-case in the other, and the rain dribbled unchecked round his neck and wrists.

'It's a dirty day, all right,' said Mr Briggs, sounding quite cheerful. 'I wondered if you'd bother coming.'

'I said I would.' The carrier-bags cut into Peter's hand, and he thought he might drop something.

'You're a good lad. We'll soon be home. The fire should be just nice when we get in.'

They turned into the yard and the wind blew the bags against Peter's wet legs as he struggled across the path to the door. When the door was opened, Peter almost fell into the hallway. He hurried into the stuffy, fetid living-room and dropped everything in a heap on the table. His hands were aching with cold, and he

stood about miserably while Mr Briggs hung up h
and filled the kettle.

'Get that wet jacket off you, son. You'll may
bit longer, till it dries. I'll make the tea. You sit
yourself.'

Peter took off his anorak and bundled it over the back of a
chair. The old man had poked the fire and put pieces of coal
round it without spoiling its blazing heart. Peter held out his
hands to it, knowing that he should have rubbed his dripping hair
and patted the wet cracks between his fingers. Already he could
feel his face becoming taut in the dry heat. He crossed to the sink,
let the water run for a minute, then put the stopper in. 'I'd better
get busy. There's a lot to do.'

Mr Briggs reached from behind him and turned off the tap.
'Nothing that won't wait, laddie. Come away from there. Just sit
down, like I said, and get this tea inside you.'

Peter sat in one of the fireside chairs with his hands wrapped
round the steaming mug. Mr Briggs brought a plate of sticky
buns and put it on the hearth near the boy.

'Mind and save some bits for Jinty. I'll let her out for a wee
flutter.' He opened the cage, but the bird remained on its perch,
singing ecstatically. He looked at the budgie fondly.

'She likes when it's raining. She knows fine we'll not rush off
and leave her.'

He held out a piece of his bun into the cage. The bird pecked it
out of his fingers, dropped it and went on singing. 'Cheeky thing!'
he said indulgently.

Peter started to drink his tea. His face was burning, and
between mouthfuls of tea and bun he hunched up first one
shoulder, then the other, and rubbed the flaming patches on his
cheeks against his rough sweater.

'What's wrong lad?'

'Nothing.'

'You don't look right. What's wrong with your face?'

'Nothing!'

Before the old man could ask any more questions, the bird
flew out of the cage and rested for a moment on Peter's head on
its way to the mantelpiece. The old man was delighted. 'Oh, I

..1ew she'd get used to you! She likes you! You'll not get rid of her next week!'

'I won't be here next week,' said Peter quietly.

'What? Why not?'

'I can't come. I won't be coming again. I'll just tidy up a bit now. Maybe during the holidays . . . ,' he said halfheartedly, while rubbing his itching hands on his trousers. He brought the carpet-sweeper out from the cupboard in the wall and pushed it around the middle of the room. Mr Briggs kept getting in the way.

'Why can't you come? Why did you come in the first place?'

'It doesn't matter.'

Peter left the sweeper standing, took a duster from under the sink and swept it smartly along the mantelpiece. The startled bird swooped round the room three times before heading for the cage. Peter's hand reached the cage door first.

'No you don't! I'm going to clean your cage properly – and you keep it clean!'

The bird sat on top of the cage looking puzzled.

'Just leave it, son. She's tired. Leave it till next week.'

'I told you! I won't be back!'

'You haven't told me much. Why are you here?'

Peter ignored him. 'I'll just give her clean water,' he said, taking the plastic bowl to the tap. The bird scrambled into the cage, and the boy replaced the bowl and shut the door.

'You should be up at the school, shouldn't you?' The old man was jubilant when he saw the change in Peter's face. 'Shouldn't you?'

'No!'

'I heard about those music lessons. Trumpets and flutes and violins. All sorts of things. And clarinets!' he added triumphantly.

'I don't have to go!'

'Aye, but that's where your Ma thinks you've gone! Isn't it?' He lifted the clarinet case from the table and thrust it under Peter's nose. The boy turned his head away.

'What happened son? Why can't you come next week? Did someone tell on you?'

'No! But I can't come back.'

Peter busied himself at the sink. He thought of all the excuses he had already given his music teacher. He thought of all the other excuses he had stored up ready, but which he could not now use because his music teacher had stopped believing him. At least he could blame the weather this week. He heard Mr Briggs opening the catches of the case and waited for the dreaded wheedling words.

'We'll surely get a tune this time, Jinty. He couldn't leave us without a tune!'

Peter clashed the dishes in the soapy water. He pulled out the stopper and piled them on the draining-board.

'C'mon son. You know how much we want to hear you play! We don't mind if you're not very good!'

Peter half-dried his sore, raw hands. He took his anorak from the chair near the fire and put it on. It steamed with his body's heat. He started to tidy the bags he had dumped on the table, first laying his music-folder on one side.

'Maybe he can't play at all, Jinty! Maybe he just carries that case because it looks nice! If he doesn't play us a tune this time, we'll never know, will we?'

The itch between Peter's fingers was unbearable. He rushed the sweeper across the room and jammed it into a corner. 'All right! All right!'

He snatched the case from the old man's hands and banged it down on the table. Deftly, he screwed the sections of the clarinet together, lining up the keys as if it was the habit of a lifetime. He took the protective metal cap off the mouthpiece, sucked the reed before positioning it and tightened the silver ligature which kept it in place. Mr Briggs was fascinated by the busy, skilful hands. He only noticed the boy's grim face when it glared redly a few inches from his own. He shrank back into his armchair.

Peter hissed at him, 'I'll give you a tune! And your stupid bird as well! You've asked for it. You'll be sorry. Here's a tune for you!'

He stuck the clarinet angrily in his mouth and blasted hard, crude notes at the old man, repeating the vulgar theme over and over like a cruel, taunting child.

Hands to his ears, Mr Briggs whimpered, 'Stop it! Oh, stop it, lad! It doesn't matter about the tune. You're frightening the bird!'

The terrified budgie was screeching and flapping, banging itself off the sides of the cage, scattering birdseed and water and tiny green feathers through the bars. Peter turned away from the old man. He blew long, unpitched rasps towards the bird, holding the clarinet in one hand while he opened the cage door with the other. He pushed the bell of the instrument into the cage, crouching level with the table on which it stood. The little quivering creature scrambled dementedly between floor and perch. It puffed out its heaving breast as if to push away the vicious, insistent tune. Mr Briggs stumbled over from his chair and pummelled Peter with his old soft fists, pleading and sobbing.

The bird was suddenly calm. It chirped once, and keeled over on its side at the bottom of the cage, one tiny eye staring beadily upwards. It gave a gentle shudder, then lay still. Peter stared in horror at the dead bird.

The old man wailed, 'You've killed her! You wee bugger! You wicked wee bugger! You've killed Jinty! Oh, the poor bird! You've killed her!'

The boy pulled the clarinet roughly out of the cage and ran out of the room and down the hallway, with the cries ringing in his ears. He ran across the yard and along the lane, ran all the way home in the driving, sleety rain. At last he stood, dripping and panting, on his doorstep and fumbled for his key. At some point he must have put the instrument inside his anorak for protection, and he realized, as his fingers touched the clammy wood, that he had left the clarinet case behind.

The wind had died and the rain was a fine drizzle when Peter went back to the house after school on Monday. He crossed the muddy yard and was relieved to find the front door unlocked and swinging slightly in the breeze. Rain had blown into the hallway. There was no rush of warmth from the living-room as he opened the door. The fire was out, a heap of fine ash spilling over on to the hearth, and the usual smells were suspended in the chill air.

The birdcage was shrouded in its flowered night-time cover.

Mr Briggs lay back in his armchair, his legs stretched stiffly in front of him, his mouth open. Peter was surprized that he was not snoring. He called his name softly. Then, since there was no answer, he tiptoed to the cluttered table and gathered up his case and his music-folder. 'Cheerio, Mr Briggs,' he said quietly. He left the cold, silent house, shutting the door behind him.

After his tea he went upstairs to his bedroom. He assembled the instrument and propped up 'Daily Exercises for the Clarinet Student' on the bookshelf. He started to practise. A family of starlings chattered and complained outside his window. Before long his eyes were filled with tears and he had to stop to blow his nose. He started playing again. The third time the music came to a sort of gurgling halt, his mother wondered downstairs if perhaps the clarinet lessons were a waste of time.

STAFF OF LIFE

Arthur Young

During the depression my father was idle. While my mother worked to keep us he ran a garden allotment, to fill his empty days, to help with food and to salve his self-respect.

It was my job to gather dung.

In the summer mornings while he bent to his weeding and hoeing, I made designs with the white chuckies which outlined the various beds; or made a wee house out of seedling boxes. Come midday we ate, sitting just inside the door of the hut which he had patiently built from boxes and old wood.

After dinner, before settling to his only pipe of the day, he would cut the heel and leaf from a stalk of red rhubarb for me. Then he puffed away, while I scrunched contentedly, dipping the end in a little poke of sugar before every bite, grooing in tart delight if I had not coated it well enough.

Soon, when his cronies came by to play solo or dominoes for spent matchsticks, they laughed at me and said it would keep me regular.

Then to be rid of me I was sent for dung, to make the flowers smell and keep the rhubarb red.

I went with Dougie Crawford, the son of one of my father's friends. He was twice my age and had a bogie.

We went to the Stey Brae, to the tracing station. On the way there I got a hurl, hunkering down on the bogie, feet on an upturned shovel. We jumbled over cobbles; swayed round corners; jinked in and out of the traffic, clear across the town to the Brae.

This hill, notorious for its steepness and twists, had running its whole length a pathway of cross-laid granite setts, to help horses keep their feet and give them purchase. At the bottom, the town council had sited a tracing station.

In a stable, by the side of the road, they kept half a dozen powerful horses. On payment of a fee by a carter, one of these would be hitched, tandem, to a heavy load, and the two horses, led by a trace boy, would plod, steaming and snorting, to the head of the hill.

Of course, the stable was a great howff. It was ruled by two ostlers, men with seamed leathery faces, who wore leggings and aprons of sacking. They had ponderous bellies, girt about with broad brass-studded leather belts. They swore at the beasts with hoarse crooning voices; roystering oaths which, I realized later, were really little songs of love.

The place would be full of drivers and carters. There would be joking, and pipe-reek, and spitting, and drinking from quart bottles of ale, while the horses were yoked and loused; fed and groomed.

The traffic on the hill was of all kinds: brewers' drays, coal lorries, grain floats, furniture pantechnicons, contractors' carts – all pulled by big, patient horses, mostly Clydesdales. There was the odd Percheron, Shire or Punch, but they weren't a patch on our local-bred beauties.

Naturally, the six trace horses were Clydesdales too. Our favourite was Hector.

Nobly named, he was the biggest by far, and was superb to see with his creamy mane against his chestnut coat, and his feet, big as pie ashets, with their silky white-fringed spats.

You can imagine our plunder was bountiful. Dougie was on to the droppings in a flash, scooping them into the bogie. Somehow, Hector's offering seemed special, as with utter disdain of the smelly, petrol-driven vehicles all about him, with their stinking exhausts, he lifted his tail and gave out great golden gobs of steaming ordure.

When we returned home, I trotted beside Dougie, holding on to his belt. As we ran we inhaled the sharp ammonia smell of our treasure.

One day a trace boy, sent for tobacco, had dawdled; was not on hand when needed.

The ostler swore.

'Whaur's yon bluidy boy got tae?'

'Can Ah go?' asked Dougie, bold and scared together.

By this time we were kenspeckle.

'Ah believe ye micht!'

Pop-eyed with pride, he took the trace bridle in his hand, then held out the other for me.

'He can come too, eh no?' he asked.

Was there ever such a hero, to remember a halfling like me in that moment of his own glory.

'Weel – ! See and haud oan tae him ticht!'

For, of course, the real reward of being a trace boy was the return journey – on the back of the horse.

We had Hector, our own beauty. He hauled the load to the top with ease, then waited patiently while the carter hefted us up on to his broad back.

Dougie held on to the big leather collar, his knuckles showing white, with me locked between his arms. Greatly daring, he dug his heels into the broad flanks. Hector obediently went forward in a slow canter.

We had so often watched the trace boys with envy, that we had never considered the danger.

The huge back was frighteningly high above the cobbles. The motion was sudden and jerky. The smooth hard coat was as slippery as glass.

Somehow we reached the other end and were helped down. Our terror turned immediately to pride and joy. Our happiness knew no limits at our own daring and success.

So the summer progressed. The flowers never smelt sweeter. The rhubarb was never so red: and I was never so regular.

When summer ended, I went to school for the first time. The allotment was forgotten in November fogs and December frosts.

There was snow, I remember, just before Christmas. One Saturday, late in the afternoon, Dougie appeared in tackety boots and a Balaclava helmet.

'Comin' tae see Hector?' he asked.

'Will I no' just!' I cried.

Without the bogie this time, we dodged along the pavements through the throng of shoppers. The winter wind dirled in my ears and to my intense excitement, before we were long on the way, it started to snow hard. This added the final touch to the twinkle of street lights in early darkness, and the bustle and smells of Christmas. I remember feeling so happy.

Landing on roads already surfaced by packed icy snow, the huge swirling flakes soon formed a muffling carpet. The heavy traffic and the countless feet pounded it hard and slippery. By the time we reached the tracing stable the Stey Brae had been converted into a dangerous glacis, under which the granite setts were buried and useless, despite attempts at clearing and sanding.

We soon caught an anxious undertone to the rough voices, for no man wanted to get in the way of the great, pounding, steel-shod hooves as they fought for surety and balance.

'Yin o' they beasts will gang doon afore ye're a' din!' warned one of the ostlers. 'They'll hae tae come aff. It's no' safe ony mair.'

But the carters already there were late and weary and wanted to get done.

'Weel! Yin mair raik an' then it's feenish!' he decreed.

Dougie and I waited confidently beside our bonny giant. He would show them.

He did too.

Stepping like the prince he was, he drove his way up the hill, hauling the yoked horse and load behind him. Dougie and I ran alongside shouting his praises.

On looking back, what made the next happening so horrifying was the incongruous silence. There was no warning horn, no squeal of brakes or tyres, no shout: just the light-beam, grotesquely out of place, shining across the road instead of down as a car slid out of control on one of the bends.

There wasn't even a very big bump, but the momentum and lack of friction underfoot was enough to sweep the cart and the two horses backwards.

For one frozen moment Hector stood his ground foursquare, until inexorably his head was pulled up, back and over. At the last moment he tried to roll sideways but his huge frame was never meant for such contortions.

'Christ! The bluidy beast is coupit,' was the agonized shout.

Then the noise started, obscene in its shrill terror. Hector lay flailing on the ground, his teeth gnashing, his eyes rolling in agony, his screams human and mortal. Jagged slivers of white bone sticking from the shin showed where the bone of the leg was broken.

One of the ostlers arrived, purple in the face.

'Aa Christ! Christ! The puir bluidy beast!'

The cry went up for a gun or for the knackers, but shaking his head the ostler drew out a horn-handled clasp knife. Opening out the big blade, he held it cupped in his hand, so that the sharp point lay sheltered and directed along his middle finger. He soothed the pain-wracked animal enough to get near it.

To my utter astonishment he lifted its tail and plunged hand, knife and arm up to the elbow into the pouting dark orifice.

'Whit's he daein' up its airse, mister?' Dougie pulled at a man's coat in alarm.

'There's a big vein in there, son. He'll puncture it, and the beast will soon be quated.'

Then more kindly: 'It'll no' hurt.'

His words seemed true, for a few minutes after the ostler brought his hand away, dripping red, the great horse quietened. His head settled and he began to breathe in ever slowing gasps.

At the end his bowels gave way and skailed a great, reeking puddle of blood in the snow, where it steamed and congealed and turned black.

I felt my head go round.

'Dougie! Take me home!'

I remember nothing of the return trip. Indeed I remember little of the next few months, except that even in those days of tight money, the doctor was called to see me.

The last time I saw Dougie Crawford was just after the start of the war.

He was a pasty-faced private in the Argylls, with black holes in his teeth and a fag stuck on his lower lip. He was killed in Malaya.

The Stey Brae has disappeared. It has been bulldozed, straightened and smoothed into a gently curving four-lane highway. Even now I can go to where Hector died.

I still get rhubarb too; sometimes with custard. But it is pale, anaemic stuff, with chlorotic leaves. They tell me it is produced in some foreign part. No doubt it is forced under glass and fed on chemical concoctions.

It only gives me wind.

SECTION II
Poetry

Vymura: the Shade Card Poem
Liz Lochhead

Now artistic I aint, but I went to choose paint
'cos the state of the place made me sick.
I got a shade card, consumers'-aid card, but it stayed hard
    to pick
So I asked her advice as to what would look nice,
would blend in and not get on my wick.

She said 'Our Vymura is super in Dürer,
or see what you think of this new shade, Vlaminck.
But I see that you're choosy . . .
Picasso is newsy . . . that's greyish-greeny-bluesy . . .
Derain's all the rage . . .
that's hot-pink and Fauve-ish . . .
There's Monet . . . that's mauve-ish . . .
And Schwitters,
that's sort-of-a *beige*.'

She said 'Fellow next door just sanded his floor
and rollered on Rouault and Rothko
His hall, och it's Pollock an' he

did his lounge in soft Hockney
with his cornice picked out in Kokoshka.'

'Now avoid the Van Gogh, you'll not get it off,
the Bonnard is bonny,
you'd be safe with matt Manet,
the Goya is *gorgeous*
or Chagall in eggshell,
but full-gloss Lautrec's sort of tacky.
So stick if you can to satin-finish Cézanne
or Constable . . . that's kind of khaki.
Or the Gainsborough green . . .
and I'd call it hooey to say Cimabue
would never tone in with Soutine.'

'If it looks a bit narrow when you splash on Pissarro,
one-coat Magritte covers over.'
She said 'This Hitchens is a nice shade for kitchens
with some Ernst to connect 'em at other end of the
    spectrum
Botticelli's lovely in the Louvre.'
She said 'If it was mine I'd do it Jim Dine . . .
don't think me élitist or snobby . . .
but Filipo Lippi'd
look awfy inspid,
especially in a large-ish lobby!'

Well, I did one wall Watteau, with the skirting Giotto
and the door and the pelmet in Poussin.
The ceiling's de Kooning,
other walls all in Hals
and the whole place looks quite . . . cavalier,
with the woodwork in Corot –
but I think tomorrow
I'll flat-white it back to Vermeer.

FAT GIRL'S CONFESSION
Liz Lochhead

Roll up and see the Fat Lady!
Such a jolly sight to see.
Seems my figure is a Figure of Fun . . .
to everyone but me.

Smile! Say Cottage Cheese!
You all know me –
I'm the Office Fat Girl, the one you see
wearing Vast Dark Dresses and a Cheery Veneer . . .
and lingerie constructed by a civil engineer.

Occasionally, you meet some bloke who'll give you this
     tripe
about how, YEUCH, he's repelled by the skinny model
     type.
He CAN'T see the attraction, he'll swear by all he owns
it'd be like lying in bed with a rickle of bones.
But, o how he LURRVES
yer Voluptuous Curves
and your Supper Board that Groans.

I met him at my wee cousin's wedding – he was the Best
     Man – he says to me
would you like to go out for a bite to eat? I mean, do you
     fancy a curry?
A Chinese? An Italian? I said, who me? Oh, I love
lasagne and canne-linguini and PASTA and stuff.
(well, who with pasta, ever says *basta*,
enough!)
And then for my MAIN course I tend to choose
something smothered in a sauce made of butter, cream and
     booze
with asparagus hollandaise and cauliflower mornay

potatoes dauphines, onion rings and mushrooms sauté.
And after the cheeseboard, my sweet tooth's nagging, so
I need another great big stodgy wedge of Black Forest
Gâteau.
Well, when it comes to pudding,
the way I see it –
with cheesecake you've a choice:
either EAT it or BE it.

I didnae cry when he left me.
I gave not one cheep, not a chirrup –
just devoured a whole packet of Mr Kipling Kunzle Cakes
and a half-hundredweight sack of Mexicali Taco Chips
dunked in maple syrup,
went for a double blackpudding supper, then half an hour later,
I ravished the refrigerator
(in my classic response to Rejection and Pain)
and immediately began eating
my Heart Out again.

But, Oh
Dear Joe,
much as I miss you
I've just been reading how Fat Is A Feminist Issue.
Fat Girls like me have all fallen from grace . . .
if I could feed my own ego I wouldnae need to feed my
face!
Everyone needs Oral Satisfaction, but
the Truly Fulfilled don't need a filled-full gut.
I says, Enough of this junk food, you are what you eat.
When did you last see your lover?
When did you last see your feet?
So . . . I'm persevering, but it's kind of hard
to live on lettuce, and self-regard.

But, you know, I've been really, really, really good today!
Breakfast was black coffee, plus a saccharine tab from the
tube.

For my lunch, a half-a-cup of chicken boullion
made with a Knorr chicken-stock cube.
Dinner: two slices of starch-reduced Ryvita
with a scrape of slimmer's imitation margarine,
then I pedalled myself blue in the face on the Exercise
    Machine.
See, I've joined this Health Club, and hell, I
saw some sights you wouldnae believe!
Enough heaving flesh to make you heave.
All that pummelling, and pedalling, and pounding, and
    sweating,
and keeking in the mirror to see how much thinner you're
    getting!
Well, there's not one lady waging the Inch War or wielding
    the tape
who doesnae wish for a Dishy Man to lick her inty shape.

So I'm stuck here in this Stephanie Bowman Sweat-It-Off
    Slimmersuit.
I feel a right clown!
I'm to huff, I'm to puff,
I'll WEAR my hips down.
I'll mortify my surplus flesh,
remove it like a tumour . . .
and all to make of myself the kind of confection
who'll appeal to the Consumer?

ALMOST MISS SCOTLAND
Liz Lochhead

The night I
Almost became Miss Scotland,
I caused a big stramash
When I sashayed on in my harristweed heathermix onepiece
And my 'Miss Garthamlock' sash.

I wis six-fit-six, I wis slinky
(Yet nae skinnymalinky) –
My waist was nipped in wi elastic,
My powder and panstick were three inches thick,
Nails? Long, blood-rid and plastic.
So my big smile'd come across, I'd larded oan lipgloss
And my false eyelashes were mink
With a sky blue crescent that was pure iridescent
When I lowered my eyelids to blink.

Well, I wiggled tapselteerie, my heels were that peerie
While a kinna Jimmy Shandish band
Played 'Flower of Scotland' –
But it aw got droont oot wi wolf whistles –
And that's no countin 'For These Are My Mountains'
– See I'd tits like nuclear missiles.

Then this familiar-lukkin felly
I'd seen a loat oan the telly
Interviewed me aboot my hobbies –
I says: Macrame, origami,
Being nice tae my mammy –
(Basically I tellt him a loat o jobbies).
I was givin it that
Aboot my ambition to chat
To handicapped and starvin children from other nations
– How I was certain I'd find

96

Travel wid broaden my mind
As I fulfilled my Miss Scotland obligations.

Well, I wis in Seventh Heaven
To be in the Final Seven –
But as the Judges retired
To do what was required
And pick the furst, second and thurd
Well, the waiting was murder and it suddenly occurred there
Was something *absurd*
Aboot the hale position
Of being in competition
Wi other burds like masel
Who I should of kennt very well
Were ma sisters (at least under the skin)
Yet fur this dubious prize I'd have scratched oot their eyes
And hoped they'd git *plooks*, so I'd win!
Aye, there wis somethin ridic'lous
Boot sookin in wi thae prickless
Wonders o judges, their 'winks' and their 'nudges'.
Wan wee baldy comedian bloke
Whose jokes were a joke:
Wan heuchter-choochter singer who wis a dead ringer
For a cross between a pig in a tartan poke
And a constipated bubblyjock:
Plus wan wellknown soak –
A member of our Sporting Fraternity
Who was guaranteed his place in Eternity
As a well-pickled former member of the Scotland Squad.
And the likes of them were Acting God,
Being Real Men,
Scoring *us* on a scale of one to ten –
They'd compare and contrast, and then at last
They'd deign to pronounce
And reverse-order-announce it.
Then I wid simper, look sweet, an
I'd burst oot greetin
Gasp 'Who me' – the usual story –

They'd plonk me down, stick on the Miss Scotland crown
To crown my crowning glory.

How would *thae guys* like to be a prize –
A cake everybody wanted a slice of –
Have every leering schoolgirl consider them a pearl
Everybody kennt the price of?
How would *they* like their mums to say that their bums
Had always attracted the Ladies' Glances,
And nothing wrang wi it, they'd aye gone alang wi it
And encouraged them to take their chances?
And they were Good Boys, their Mum's Pride & Joys,
Saving it for their Future Wives?
And despite their fame they still steyed at hame
And lived real clean-living lives?

In a blinding flash I saw the hale thing was trash
– I just Saw Rid
And here's whit I did

– Now I'd love to report that I was the sort
To speak out and convince the other lassies
Pick bones wi aw the chaperones
And singlehandedly convert the masses
Till in a bacchanalian Revenge of the Barbie Dolls
Crying 'All for One and One for All!'
We advanced on the stage, full of bloodlust and rage –
But, I cannot tell a lie, the truth is that I
Just stuck on my headsquerr and snuck away oot o therr –
I know I did right, it wisnae contrary –
And I let my oaxters grow back in
Really rid and thick and hairy.

Because the theory of feminism's aw very well
But yiv got tae see it fur yirsel
Every individual hus tae realize
Her hale fortune isnae in men's eyes,
Say enough is enough
Away and get stuffed.

FOUR OF THE BELT
Tom Leonard

Jenkins, all too clearly it is time
for some ritual physical humiliation;
and if you cry, boy, you will prove
what I suspect – you are not a man.

As they say, Jenkins, this hurts me
more than it hurts you. But I show you
I am a man, by doing this, to you.

When *you* are a man, Jenkins, you may hear
that physical humiliation and ritual
are concerned with strange adult matters
– like rape, or masochistic fantasies.

You will not accept such stories.
Rather, you will recall with pride,
perhaps even affection, that day when I,
Mr Johnstone, summoned you before me,
and gave you four of the belt

like this. And this. And this. And this.

MORAL PHILOSOPHY
Tom Leonard

whiji *mean* whiji mean

lissn
noo lissnty mi toknty yi
right

h hawd oan
whair wuzza
naw

aye
whitsiz name
him way thi
yi no yon

here
here yoo
yir no eevn lissnin
name a god

a doant no

MR ENDREWS SPEAKS
Tom Leonard

(The following short scene takes place in St Kevin Barry's, a large school in Glasgow. Over the tannoy, which has speakers in every classroom, comes the voice of Mr Andrews, the new headmaster. He speaks with a Kelvinside accent.)
This is your headmester speaking. This is Mr Endrews, your new headmester. I want to make one thing clear above all. It is my determination to make St Kevin Berry's a school of which the city of Glesgow cen be justly proud. This city of Glesgow, the envy of Europe for its many beautiful perks. Why only the other day in one of these beautiful perks, Kelvingrove, I chenced across a former pupil of this very school, who enswered to the name of 'Tcm'. Now Tcm, I could see, was thinking long thoughts over a small bottle of hair lecquer. Beside him on his bench lay one of his unfortunate pals, who had some hours before shaken off this mortal coil. Rigor mortis was complete, end his right hend was set in what is known es 'a messonic hendshake'. 'Tem,' I said severely, 'hev you been freternizing with those of another Faith?' But Tem slid forward from his bench, end went to join his hepless friend in thet lend from whose bourn no treveller returns.

Now Tem was never one to hev known the dignity of a laudable profession with a substantial celery, like my own. It was his own fault, of course. Et St Kevin Berry's he would hev the school motto, 'Porridge end the Tawse' inscribed on all his Eff Two's. But a lack of self-discipline was to prove his downfall in later years. You know, my feather was gerrotted when I was a child end it didn't do *me* any herm. No, I stuck herd et my studies, end in the fullness of time became a gredduate of Glesgow University. End there were no State hendouts in my day, one hed to get by on a seck of oats. *(Clears his throat.)* A seck of oats.

Of course none of you listening to me here this morning will ever go to Glesgow University, I'm aware of thet. Most of you will be in the hends of the Glesgow constebulary before very long, end some of you will no doubt make your appearance in the High

101

Court on a cherge of murder. Now I want you to hev the honour of St Kevin Berry's in mind when you plead guilty, end under no circumstences should you use the glottal stop. I want you all to say, 'Guilty,' in a clear, well-mennered voice, with no trace of slovenly speech.

Teachers. Efter this address, all clesses will prectise saying 'Guilty' for thirty minutes. Tomorrow morning et 9 am sherp I will make a rendom inspection, end any boy who uses the glottal stop in reply to my question, 'How do you plead?' will be for six of the belt. With my new Lochgelly, which can stend on its own.

Finally. You will no doubt be aware thet with the coming of spring, it is no longer derk between the hours of four end five. This means thet I will be doubly severe with those pupils caught urinating in the hedges of local gerdens on the way home from school. If pupils behave like sevages, they will be sevagely dealt with.

Now I want Thomas Meguire end Frencis Lawson of Four Zed in my office et once. Sherp.

THE ADOPTION PAPERS
Jackie Kay

CHAPTER 6: THE TELLING PART

Ma mammy bot me oot a shop
Ma mammy says I was a luvly baby

Ma mammy picked me (I wiz the best)
your mammy had to take you (she'd no choice)

Ma mammy says she's no really ma mammy
(just kid on)

It's a bit like a part you've rehearsed so well
you can't play it on the opening night
She says my real mammy is away far away
Mammy why aren't you and me the same colour
But I love my mammy whether she's real or no
My heart started rat tat tat like a tin drum
all the words took off to another planet
Why

But I love ma mammy whether she's real or no

I could hear the upset in her voice
I says *I'm not your real mother*,
though Christ knows why I said that,
If I'm not who is, but all my planned speech
went out the window

She took me when I'd nowhere to go
my mammy is the best mammy in the world OK.
After mammy telt me she wisnae my real mammy
I was scared to death she was gonnie melt
or something or mibbe disappear in the dead
of night and somebody would say she wis a fairy

103

godmother. So the next morning I felt her skin
to check it was flesh, but mibbe it was just
a good imitation. How could I tell if my mammy
was a dummy with a voice spoken by someone else?
So I searches the whole house for clues
but I never found nothing. Anyhow a day after
I got my guinea pig and forgot all about it.

I always believed in the telling anyhow.
You can't keep something like that secret
I wanted her to think of her other mother
out there, thinking that child I had will be
seven today eight today all the way up to
god knows when. I told my daughter –
I bet your mother's never missed your birthday,
how could she?

Mammy's face is cherries.
She is stirring the big pot of mutton soup
singing *I gave my love a cherry*
it had no stone.
I am up to her apron.
I jump onto her feet and grab her legs
like a huge pair of trousers,
she walks round the kitchen lifting me up.

Suddenly I fall off her feet.
And mammy falls to the floor.
She won't stop the song
I gave my love a chicken it had no bone.
I run next door for help.
When me and Uncle Alec come back
Mammy's skin is toffee stuck to the floor.
And her bones are all scattered like toys.

Now when people say 'ah but
it's not like having your own child though is it',
I say of course it is, what else is it?

she's my child, I have told her stories
wept at her losses, laughed at her pleasures,
she is mine.

I was always the first to hear her in the night
all this umbilical knot business is nonsense
– the men can afford deeper sleeps that's all.
I listened to hear her talk,
and when she did I heard my voice under hers
and now some of her mannerisms crack me up

Me and my best pal
don't have Donny Osmond or David Cassidy
on our walls and we don't wear Starsky and Hutch
jumpers either. Round at her house we put on
the old record player and mime to Pearl Bailey
Tired of the life I lead, tired of the blues I breed
and Bessie Smith I can't do without my kitchen man.
Then we practise ballroom dancing giggling,
everyone thinks we're dead old-fashioned.

CHAPTER 7: BLACK BOTTOM

Maybe that's why I don't like
all this talk about her being black,
I brought her up as my own
as I would any other child
colour matters to the nutters;
but she says my daughter says
it matters to her

I suppose there would have been things
I couldn't understand with any child,
we knew she was coloured.
They told us they had no babies at first
and I chanced it didn't matter what colour it was
and they said *oh well are you sure*
in that case we have a baby for you –

105

to think she wasn't even thought of as a baby,
my baby, my baby

I chase his *Sambo Sambo* all the way from the school gate.
A fistful of anorak – What did you call me? Say that again.
Sam-bo. He plays the word like a bouncing ball
but his eyes move fast as ping pong.
I shove him up against the wall,
say that again you wee shite. *Sambo, sambo*, he's crying now

I knee him in the balls. What was that?
My fist is steel; I punch and punch his gut.
Sorry I didn't hear you? His tears drip like wax.
Nothing he heaves *I didn't say nothing*.
I let him go. He is a rat running. He turns
and shouts *Dirty Darkie* I chase him again.
Blonde hairs in my hand. Excuse me!
This teacher from primary 7 stops us.
Names? I'll report you to the headmaster tomorrow.
But Miss. Save it for Mr Thompson she says

My teacher's face cracks into a thin smile
Her long nails scratch the note well well
I see you were fighting yesterday, again.
In a few years' time you'll be a juvenile delinquent.
Do you know what that is? Look it up in the dictionary.
She spells each letter with slow pleasure.
Read it out to the class.
Thug. Vandal. Hooligan. Speak up. Have you lost your tongue?

To be honest I hardly ever think about it
except if something happens, you know
daft talk about darkies. Racialism.
Mothers ringing my bell with their kids
crying *You tell. You tell. You tell.*
– *No*. You tell your little girl to stop calling
my little girl names and I'll tell my little girl
to stop giving your little girl a doing.

We're practising for the school show
I'm trying to do the Cha Cha and the Black Bottom
but I can't get the steps right
my right foot's left and my left foot's right
my teacher shouts from the bottom
of the class Come on, show

us what you can do I thought
you people had it in your blood.
My skin is hot as burning coal
like that time she said Darkies are like coal
in front of the whole class – my blood
what does she mean? I thought

she'd stopped all that after the last time
my dad talked to her on parents' night
the other kids are all right till she starts;
my feet step out of time, my heart starts
to miss beats like when I can't sleep at night –
What Is In My Blood? The bell rings, it is time.

Sometimes it is hard to know what to say
that will comfort. Us two in the armchair;
me holding her breath, 'they're ignorant
let's have some tea and cake, forget them'.

Maybe it's really Bette Davis I want
to be the good twin or even better the bad
one or a nanny who drowns a baby in a bath.
I'm not sure maybe I'd prefer Katharine
Hepburn tossing my red hair, having a hot
temper. I says to my teacher Can't I be
Elizabeth Taylor, drunk and fat and she
just laughed, not much chance of that.
I went for an audition for *The Prime
of Miss Jean Brodie*. I didn't get a part
even though I've been acting longer
than Beverley Innes. So I have. Honest.

Olubayo was the colour of peat
when we walked out heads turned
like horses, folk stood like trees
their eyes fixed on us – it made me
burn, that hot glare; my hand
would sweat down to his bone.
Finally, alone, we'd melt
nothing, nothing would matter

He never saw her. I looked for him in her;
for a second it was as if he was there
in that glass cot looking back through her.

On my bedroom wall is a big poster
of Angela Davis who is in prison
right now for nothing at all
except she wouldn't put up with stuff.
My mum says she is *only* 26
which seems really old to me
but my mum says it is young

just imagine, she says, being on
America's Ten Most Wanted People's List at 26!
I can't.
Angela Davis is the only female person
I've seen (except for a nurse on TV)
who looks like me. She had big hair like mine
that grows out instead of down.
My mum says it's called an *Afro*.
If I could be as brave as her when I get older
I'll be OK.
Last night I kissed her goodnight again
and wondered if she could feel the kisses
in prison all the way from Scotland.
Her skin is the same too you know.
I can see my skin is that colour
but most of the time I forget,
so sometimes when I look in the mirror

I give myself a bit of a shock
and say to myself *Do you really look like this?*
as if I'm somebody else. I wonder if she does that.

I don't believe she killed anybody.
It is all a load of phoney lies.
My dad says it's a set up.
I asked him if she'll get the electric chair
like them Roseberries he was telling me about.
No he says the world is on her side.
Well how come she's in there then I thinks.
I worry she's going to get the chair.
I worry she's worrying about the chair.
My dad says she'll be putting on a brave face.
He brought me a badge home which I wore
to school. It says FREE ANGELA DAVIS.
And all my pals says 'Who's she?'

MY GRANDMOTHER'S HOUSES
Jackie Kay

1

She is on the second floor of a tenement
From her front room window you see the cemetery

Her bedroom is my favourite: newspapers
dating back to the War covering every present
she's ever got since the War. What's the point
in buying her anything my mother moans.
Does she use it. Does she even look at it.
I spend hours unwrapping and wrapping endless
tablecloths, napkins, perfume, bath salts,
stories of things I can't understand, words
like conscientious objector. At night I climb
over all the newspaper parcels to get to bed,
harder than the school's obstacle course. High up
in her bed all the print merges together.

When she gets the letter she is hopping mad.
What does she want with anything modern,
a shiny new pin? Here is home.
The sideboard solid as a coffin.
The newsagents next door which sells
hazelnut toffees and her *Daily Record*.
Chewing for ages over the front page,
her toffees sticking to her false teeth.

2

The new house is called a high rise.
I play in the lift all the way up to 24.
Once I get stuck for a whole hour.
From her window you see noisy kids
playing hopscotch or home.

She makes endless pots of vegetable soup,
a big bit of hoch floating inside like a fish

Till finally she gets to like the hot
running water in her own bathroom
the wall-to-wall foam-backed carpet
the parcels locked in her air-raid shelter.
But she still doesn't settle down;
even at 70 she cleans people's houses
for ten bob and goes to church on Sundays,
dragging me along to the strange place where the air
is trapped and ghosts sit at the altar.
My parents do not believe. It is down to her.
A couple of prayers. A hymn or two.
Threepenny bit in the collection hat.
A flock of women in coats and fussy hats
flapping over me like missionaries, and that is that,
until the next time God grabs me in Glasgow with Gran.

3
By the time I am seven we are almost the same height.
She still walks faster, rushing me down the High Street
till we get to her cleaning house. The hall is huge.
Rooms lead off like an octopus's arms.
I sit in a room with a grand piano, top open –
a one-winged creature, whilst my gran polishes
for hours. Finally bored I start to pick some notes
oh can you wash a sailor's shirt oh can you wash and clean
till my gran comes running, duster in hand.
I told you don't touch anything. The woman comes too;
the posh one all smiles that make goosepimples
run up my arms. Would you like to sing me a song?
Someone's crying my Lord Kumbaya. Lovely, she says,
beautiful child, skin the colour of café au lait.
'Café oh what? Hope she's not being any bother.'
Not at all. Not at all. You just get back to your work.
On the way back to her high rise I see her

like the hunchback of Notre Dame. Everytime I crouch
over a comic she slaps me. Sit up straight.

She is on the ground floor of a high rise.
From her living-room you see ambulances,
screaming their way to the Royal Infirmary.

EUGENESIS
William McIlvanney

On the first day they eradicated war.
Nations were neutralized. In desert places
The cumbered void rusted with defused bombs,
The gutted chambers. In random heaps
The rockets lay, like molar monuments
To brontosauri sentenced to extinction.

On the second day They fed the starving.
The capsules gave immunity from hunger.
Faces filled. The smiles were uniform.
The computers had found a formula for plenty.

The third day ended work. With summer
Processed to a permanence, the sun-
Machine in operation, every day
Would be as long as They desired it.
Season-chambers were erected. The nostalgic
Could take a holiday to autumn if they wished.
The computers thought of everything.

On the fourth day death was dead.
Synthetic hearts, machine-tooled brains,
Eyes and limbs were all expendable.
Immortality came wrapped in polythene.
Every face was God's you saw upon the street.

By the fifth day crime was cured.
Mind-mechanics, They located every hatred,
Extracted it, and amputated angers.
Each idea was sterilized before its issue.
The computers fixed a safety-mark for thinking.

The sixth day saw heaven's inauguration.
Benignity pills were issued. Kindness meetings
Were held on every corner. They declared
Love as the prerogative of all.
That day became the longest there had been.
But as long as there was light the people smiled.

On the seventh day, while They were resting
A small man with red hair had disappeared.
A museum missed a tent. Neither was found.
He left an immortal wife, the changeless years
Of endless happiness, and a strange note
In ancient script, just four historic letters.
The Autotongue translated: 'Irrational Anger.'
The Medic Machine advised: 'Rejection Symptoms.
Source Unknown. Primordial and Contagious.'

It was too late. The word ran like a rash
On walls and daubed on doorways. Cities emptied.
In panic They neglected Their machines.
The sunset was unauthorized. Its beauty
Triggered the light-oriented metal cocks
That crew until their mechanisms burst.
Fires twinkled in the new night, shaping mattocks.
On the dark hills an unheavenly sound was heard.
The Historometer intoned into the silence:
'Ancient Barbaric Custom Known as Laughter.'
Seizing up, the computers began to cry.

INITIATION
William McIlvanney

In shadowed and red-curtained room
My father talked towards his death
While birds made morning in the sky
And children laughed his death a lie
And each sun on the window-pane
Asked him would they meet again?
And I sat with him in the room,
Listened, nodded, laughed and talked
And brought him living words that mocked
The lonely, leafless road he walked.
He watched us distant, passing by.
Alone my father had to die.

Words withered in the barren breath.
Friends gathered in his lonely place,
Stood hope to hope and could not stop
Death closing on my father's face.
Love's bleeding fingers could not break
The way my father had to take.

Oh how time held us in his fist
And forced us to a helpless close,
Took a night, a room, a drifting mist
And nailed them on my father's life.
The cancer rotting in the lung
Cared not how many hands were wrung.

Then let me not take sackcloth for my grief
Or hang the hungry lashes with my tears.
This man went as quiet as a leaf,
Dumb as a lily in the singing years.
The wind in harebells will ring loud enough.
Nothing. Nothing. Nothing is enough.

NOT THE BURRELL COLLECTION
Edwin Morgan

The Buenos Aires Vase, one mile across,
flickering with unsleeping silent flames,
its marble carved in vine-leaves mixed with names,
shirtless ones and *desaparecidos*;
a collier's iron collar, riveted,
stamped by his Burntisland owner; a spade
from Babiy Yar; a blood-crust from the blade
that jumped the corpse of Wallace for his head;
the stout rack soaked in Machiavelli's sweat;
a fire-circled scorpion; a blown frog;
the siege of Beirut in stained glass; a sift
of Auschwitz ash; an old tapestry-set
unfinished, with a crowd, a witch, a log;
a lachrymatory no man can lift.

THE GLASGOW SUBWAY POEMS
Edwin Morgan

THE BUDGIE

Spirit of the place,
mascot of the enterprise,
lurking in the tunnels,
flashing past windows
or riding on the roof,
perky yet shy,
talkative but elusive,
she's a ball of gold
like a light's reflection,
a chatterbox
you think you heard
but turn your paper
and shake your head
as the train gathers speed.
The guard is her friend
and drops a few crumbs.
She picks, pecks, turns,
a magic bird,
a clockwork orange.

THE CAT

The subway cat
just loves to sing.
You cannot miss him
as he struts on the platform
in his red leather boots,
inflating his chest
and stroking his whiskers,
gets the key on his moothie
and renders his favourites,
'O Flower of Cessnock'
and 'Hillhead the Brave'.
Girls come to pat him,
boys shake his paw,
and once he was kidnapped
by an impresario
from Bakerloo
but he sprang his basket
and soon he was back
to yodel at West Street
and dance at Cowcaddens.

117

THE GIRAFFE

The subway giraffe
keeps its head down.
It has a special joint
in its neck. Its mother
is known to have been friendly
with an excavator.
It feeds on old tickets,
a cold chip or two,
makes do with cigarette-ends
but shivers with pleasure
at a scatter of rings
torn off from cans,
smacks its lips
as the metal rattles
down to its stomach.
The neighbours nod wisely:
'Favours his da.'

THE PIRANHAS

Did anyone tell you
that in each subway train
there is one special seat
with a small hole in it
and underneath the seat
is a tank of piranha-fish
which have not been fed
for quite some time.
The fish become agitated
by the shoogling of the train
and jump up through the seat.
The resulting skeletons
of unlucky passengers
turn an honest penny
for the transport executive,
hanging far and wide
in medical schools.

AFTER THE WAR
Douglas Dunn

The soldiers came, brewed tea in Snoddy's field
Beside the wood from where we watched them pee
In Snoddy's stagnant pond, small boys hidden
In pines and firs. The soldiers stood or sat
Ten minutes in the field, some officers apart
With the select problems of a map. Before,
Soldiers were imagined, we were them, gunfire
In our mouths, most cunning local skirmishers.
Their sudden arrival silenced us. I lay down
On the grass and saw the blue shards of an egg
We'd broken, its warm yolk on the green grass,
And pine cones like little hand grenades.

One burst from an imaginary Browning,
A grenade well thrown by a child's arm,
And all these faces like our fathers' faces
Would fall back bleeding, trucks would burst in flames,
A blood-stained map would float on Snoddy's pond.
Our ambush made the soldiers laugh, and some
Made booming noises from behind real rifles
As we ran among them begging for badges,
Our plimsolls on the fallen May-blossom
Like boots on the faces of dead children.
But one of us had left. I saw him go
Out through the gate, I heard him on the road
Running to his mother's house. They lived alone,
Behind a hedge round an untended garden
Filled with broken toys, abrasive loss;
A swing that creaked, a rusted bicycle.
He went inside just as the convoy passed.

WASHING THE COINS
Douglas Dunn

You'd start at seven, and then you'd bend your back
Until they let you stand up straight, your hands
Pressed on your kidneys as you groaned for lunch,
Thick sandwiches in grease-proofed bundles, piled
Beside the jackets by the hawthorn hedges.
And then you'd bend your little back again
Until they let you stand up straight. Your hands,
On which the earth had dried in layers, itched, itched,
Though worse still was that ache along the tips
Of every picking finger, each broken nail
That scraped the ground for sprawled potatoes
The turning digger churned out of the drills.
Muttering strong Irish men and women worked
Quicker than local boys. You had to watch them.
They had the trick of sideways-bolted spuds
Fast to your ear, and the upset wire basket
That broke your heart but made the Irish laugh.
You moaned, complained, and learned the rules of work.
Your boots, enlarging as the day wore on,
Were weighted by the magnets of the earth,
And rain in the face was also to have
Something in common with bedraggled Irish.
You held your hands into the rain, then watched
Brown water drip along your chilling fingers
Until you saw the colour of your skin
Through rips disfiguring your gloves of mud.
It was the same for everyone. All day
That bead of sweat tickled your smeared nose
And a glance upwards would show you trees and clouds
In turbulent collusions of the sky
With ground and ground with sky, and you portrayed
Among the wretched of the native earth.
Towards the end you felt you understood

The happy rancour of the Irish howkers.
When dusk came down, you stood beside the byre
For the farmer's wife to pay the labour off.
And this is what I remember by the dark
Whitewash of the byre wall among shuffling boots.
She knew me, but she couldn't tell my face
From an Irish boy's, and she apologized
And roughed my hair as into my cupped hands
She poured a dozen pennies of the realm
And placed two florins there, then cupped her hands
Around my hands, like praying together.
It is not good to feel you have no future.
My clotted hands turned coins to muddy copper.
I tumbled all my coins upon our table.
My mother ran a basin of hot water.
We bathed my wages and we scrubbed them clean.
Once all that sediment was washed away,
That residue of field caked on my money,
I filled the basin to its brim with cold;
And when the water settled I could see
Two English kings among their drowned Britannias.

THE SCOTTISH SONG
Adam McNaughtan

When the Scots had smashed the Norsemen, like steelies against
    jauries,
The Generals, Macbeth and Banquo, walked it back to Forres.
They met three dames that did a kinna fortune-tellin thing.
Who hailt Macbeth an tellt him he'd be Cawdor, Glamis an
    King.
Then Macbeth fell in a dwam but Banquo says, 'Haud on a wee.
Ye've a loat to say to him, huv ye got anyhin for me?'
The witches said, 'The good news first an then the bad we'll tell:
Ye'll faither mony kings but ye'll no be wan yersel.'
    When the King said, 'You're the hauder
        O the title Thane o Cawdor'.
        Macbeth wis fair excitit an ambitious to get oan.
        But his jaw near hut the flair
        When he heard the King declare:
        'Ma boay's the Prince o Cumberland an heir to the
           throne.'

Macbeth raced hame to Inverness an oor afore the rest
An he tellt his wife the King wis comin there to be their guest.
She says, 'Ye're mad to say it or else Duncan's aff his heid,
Cause if he sleeps here the night he's gonnae waken up deid.'
Then Macbeth convinced himsel that his motives were the best:
That he widnae murder Duncan as his cousin, king an guest.
'You're a coward, you don't love me, you're nae sodger!' says his
    wife,
'An we'll blame it oan the guairds.' Says he, 'Juist ca' me Mac the
Knife.'
    So he killt Duncan
    An his Lady smeart the drunken
    Guairds wi bluid an says, 'C'moan to bed. It's easy as
        snuff.'
    But Malcolm shot the craw,

So did Donalbain an a',
An they didnae baffle Banquo an they didnae fool
Macduff.

So Macbeth invitit Banquo to a feast as guest o honour,
Eftir hirin three miscreants to make sure he was a goner.
An at the feast he simpert aboot Banquo no bein there
But then he hud to staun cause Banquo's ghost was in his chair.
But whit made him loass his marbles was when wan o the
miscreants
Came an said they'd malkied Banquo but they'd missed the
fleein Fleance.
'Avaunt!' he starts but Lady Mac says, 'Folks, the party's closed.
An ye must excuse ma husband, he's a wee bit indisposed.'
      The threat o Fleance oan the throne juis'
      So obsessed his haill subcoanscious
      That he ordert them to kill Macduff's wife, weans, cats,
         dugs – the lot.
      Lady Mac says, 'Ah must try
      If anything that Ah can buy,
      Persil, Ariel, Daz or Flash'll shift this bluidy spot.'

But Macduff was aff to England for to fetch back Malkie
An the boay says, 'Ah'm nae use, juist a randy, greedy alkie.'
Cries Macduff, 'Ma hope ends here!' Malkie says, 'Ah'm only
kiddin,
Ah'll take an army north an cut doon leaves to keep it hidden.'
Macbeth meanwhile decidit the weird sisters he'd get haud ae.
An he fund them makin broth wi Tartars' lips to gie it body.
An they tellt him he could not be killt by man that's born o
wumman
An he didnae need to fear till he saw Birnam wuid was comin.
      So Macbeth became quite gallus
      But he'd nothing left but malice
      He couldnae show emotions like compassion, joy or
         sorrow.
      When he heard his wife had died

He juist said, 'Ah wid've cried
If it had been the morra an the morra an the morra.'

Though a' his pals hud skied it, he was safe in Dunsinane
An he passed the time by pittin armour oan an aff again.
Then the news that Birnam wuid was oan the march gied him a
scare.
He says, 'We'll fight ootside, Ah don't want bluid a' ower ma
flair.'
He wis swashin, he wis bucklin, he talked Siward's boay to
death,
But his coanfidence was shattert when Macduff shouts, 'Heh
Macbeth!'
'Against men o weemen born,' he says, 'Ah've goat divine
protection.'
Quips Macduff, 'Ah was delivert by Caesarian section.'
 Then Macduff cut aff his heid
 An when he saw that he was deid,
 Malky says, 'Yese a' are earls, the first there's ever been.'
 That's the story at an end
 But Ah still cannae comprehend
 Whit thae teachers find sae funny in yon porter scene.

OOR HAMLET
Adam McNaughtan

There was this king sleeping in his gairden a' alane
When his brither in his ear drapped a wee tait o' henbane.
Then he stole his brither's crown and his money and his
   widow
But the deid king walked and goat his son and said, 'Heh,
   listen, kiddo!'
'Ah've been killt and it's your duty to take revenge oan
   Claudius.
Kill him quick and clean and show the nation whit a fraud
   he is.'
The boay says, 'Right, Ah'll dae it, but Ah'll huvti play it
   crafty.
So that naeb'dy will suspect me, Ah'll kid oan that Ah'm a
   daftie.'

So wi' a' except Horatio (and he trusts him as a friend),
Hamlet – that's the boay – kids oan he's roon the bend,
And because he wisnae ready for obligatory killing
He tried to make the king think he was tuppence aff the
   shilling;
Took the mickey oot Polonius, treatit poor Ophelia vile,
And tellt Rosencrantz and Guildenstern that Denmark was
   a jile.
Then a troupe o' travelling actors, like 7.84
Arrived to dae a special wan-night gig in Elsinore.

   Hamlet, Hamlet! Loved his mammy.
   Hamlet, Hamlet! Acting balmy.
   Hamlet, Hamlet! Hesitating.
   Wonders if the ghost's a cheat and that is why he's
      waiting.

125

Then Hamlet wrote a scene for the players to enact,
While Horatio and him would watch to see if Claudius
    cracked.
The play was ca'd 'The Mousetrap', (No the wan that's
    running noo)
And sure enough, the king walked oot afore the scene was
    through.
So Hamlet's goat the proof that Claudius gied his da the dose,
The only problem being noo that Claudius knows he
    knows.
So while Hamlet tells his ma that her new husband's no a
    fit wan,
Uncle Claud pits oot a contract wi' the English King as
    hit-man.

And when Hamlet killed Polonius, the concealed corpus
    delecti
Was the king's excuse to send him for an English hempen
    necktie,
Wi' Rosencrantz and Guildenstern to make sure he goat
    there,
But Hamlet jumped the boat and pit the finger oan that
    pair.
Meanwhile, Laertes heard his da had been stabbed through
    the arras;
He came racing back to Elsinore toute-suite, hot-foot fae
    Paris.
And Ophelia, wi' her da killt by the man she wished to
    marry –
Efter saying it wi' flooers, she committit hari-kari.

    Hamlet, Hamlet! Nae messin!
    Hamlet, Hamlet! Learnt his lesson.
    Hamlet, Hamlet! Yorick's crust
    Convinced him that men, good or bad, at last must
        come to dust.

Then Laertes loast the place and was demanding
retribution,
But the king said, 'Keep the heid and Ah'll provide ye a
solution.'
And he arranged a sword-fight wi' the interestit perties,
Wi' a bluntit sword for Hamlet and a shairp sword for
Laertes.
And to make things double-sure – the auld belt and braces
line –
He fixed a poisont sword-tip and a poisont cup o' wine,
And the poisont sword goat Hamlet but Laertes went and
muffed it,
'Cause he goat stabbed hissel and he confessed afore he
snuffed it.

Then Hamlet's mammy drank the wine and as her face
turnt blue,
Hamlet says, 'Ah quite believe the king's a baddy noo.'
'Incestuous, murd'rous, damned Dane,' he said, to be
precise,
And made up for hesitating by killing Claudius twice;
'Cause he stabbed him wi' the sword and forced the wine
atween his lips
Then he said, 'The rest is silence.' That was Hamlet hud his
chips.
They fired a volley ower him that shook the topmost rafter
And Fortinbras, knee-deep in Danes, lived happy ever
after.

> Hamlet, Hamlet! Aw the gory!
> Hamlet, Hamlet! End of story.
> Hamlet, Hamlet! Ah'm away!
> If you think this is boring, you should read the bloody
> play!

Exploring the texts

The Ferry

One of the themes of this story is the comic way in which young children see and understand the world around about them. Aleck and Joe enjoy 'making believe' about exciting people and places in their adventures. However, reality and security for them is being at home in Govan – as they discover too late.

Suggestion for writing
Write a critical response to 'The Ferry' that gives a brief account of the story and then goes on to show how the author deals with the fantasies and realities of children's lives.

◆ Keep the account of the story short – say who wrote it; where it is set; who is in it; and what happens in it.
◆ Consider the boys' fantasy adventures – the jungle; REAL Indians; hunting; cannibals; dogging school forever; Louie in the chip shop; hijacking the ferry to Africa or America.
◆ Look carefully at the skilful and amusing way in which these childish ideas are expressed. Give quotes from the story to illustrate your points.
◆ Consider the reality the boys encounter – the pigeon fancier's threat; mucky, tarry hands; the hostility of unfamiliar territory;

being barred by the ferry pilot; Bloody Partick.

◆ Look carefully at how the author uses different words and images to contrast the unpleasant reality with the boys' make believe. Again, give quotes from the story to illustrate what you mean.

◆ Write a final paragraph that sums up how the story has accurately, and humorously, shown how children understand only part of the world around them.

Blood

In pairs

◆ Write down as many sayings or expressions as you can think of which include the word 'blood'.

◆ Now try to think of the reasons the author might have had for choosing 'Blood' as the title for this story. There may be more than one reason.

◆ Make a list of all the 'romantic' or fantasy ideas Martin has before he goes to Ireland. Opposite that, make a list of the 'realities' he discovers.

Group discussion

First, try to find out as much as you can about the background to the troubles in Northern Ireland. Then begin your discussion by asking each person in the group which of the following statements he or she would agree with:

— If the only way to gain independence for Scotland was to be like Michael or Peter, it wouldn't be worth it.

— Any war in which children are killed is wrong.

— The troubles In Northern Ireland show that religion causes nothing but trouble.

Suggestion for writing – Diary Entry

Imagine that Martin keeps a diary. Write up his account of the day he spends in Belfast. Start with his feelings and expectations as he steps off the boat. Show his changing mood as he walks through Timothy's neighbourhood and goes to the pub. Try to bring out all the fears and emotions he experiences throughout the incident in the pub, and his feelings as he watches his uncle being confronted by the two men. Finish with Martin's reflections about Timothy, now that he knows the truth, and his thoughts about Belfast, the Irish struggle, and his own home town, Glasgow.

The Great McGunnigle

'The Great McGunnigle' is an example of what is known as a sting-in-the-tail story, which means that the ending comes as a surprise to the reader. It is also a certain kind of sting-in-the-tail story in that it depends for its effect on the reader being misled until the very end. You may have read other stories that use a similar idea. A familiar, perhaps overworked, variation is the kind of story in which we are unaware until the end that the main character is actually a dog or a cat. When using this technique, the story-teller, while hoping to mislead the reader, must try not to 'cheat,' i.e. all the details should fit both the truth and the deception. Sometimes, the main interest of such stories is the trick storytelling itself.

Discussion – In pairs
◆ Do you think there are other points of interest in this story apart from the trick? For example, does the writer use the device to put across ideas about school life?
◆ Are there any points in the story where you think the writer might be 'cheating'?

Role-play
Imagine a scene in the Milloy household, when Milloy brings Greta home after the Hallowe'en dance. Mrs Milloy is at home alone. Over coffee, Greta and Milloy speak angrily about McGunnigle's behaviour, and Mrs Milloy recalls the incident at the school fête. They are in full flight, discussing McGunnigle and what should be done about him, when Mr Milloy enters.

Act out the scene, remembering that Mr and Mrs Milloy have differing attitudes towards their son.

Suggestion for writing – Point of View
Suppose the headmaster is interviewing McGunnigle, trying to find out what led to the incident between him and Milloy. McGunnigle

gives his version of what happened, plus accounts of the Hallowe'en party, the school fête, the football match, the trouble about homework, and the final confrontation.

Write down what McGunnigle says, beginning, 'Well, Sir, Mr Milloy has always seemed to pick on me . . . '. Continue the piece as a monologue, i.e. give only McGunnigle's side of the conversation.

First Foot

Discussion – In pairs
Discuss what you think of the characters.

Janice
What do you like about her? What are you less keen about? Could she do anything else to get on with her mother? Why can't she express her love for her mother? Is there any other way she could deal with Irene? Should she continue her relationship with Joe? Would you leave home if you were in her place?

Janice's mother
What is her problem regarding Janice? Why do you think she gets so annoyed? Is there any justification for her anger? Has she the right to expect Janice to stay home with her more?

Joe
What do you like about Joe? Is he good for Janice? Should he encourage her to stay at home?

Role-play
Role-play the following situations, which involve either two or three people:

◆ You have been out later than you should have been. You know your mother will be waiting up for you, and you know she might be annoyed. You ask a friend to come back with you for a cup of coffee and to watch the late film, so that your mother will not be able to get at you. But, when you go in, she starts on at you.

◆ You come through for your breakfast and discover that your mother is paying for your brother to go on an adventure holiday when she has recently refused to give you money for something you want. You ask for an explanation.

◆ Your divorced mother is going out to the pub with someone you don't like. She knows you don't like him, but she still wants to go. While she is getting ready, you can't resist giving your point of view.

Suggestion for writing – Letter to a Problem Page

Janice decides to write a letter to a problem page, seeking advice about her relationships with her mother and her sister, Irene, and about whether or not she should go back home. She needs to sort out her feelings, and her thoughts about who's to blame; she wants explanations, and advice for the future.

Write Janice's letter and then compose the agony aunt's reply. Alternatively, swap letters with someone else in the class and reply to their letter.

A Picture of Zoe

In Groups

In this story we are presented with at least two views of the main character, Zoe. Either *improvise* or *script* the following scenes that will illustrate these two views of her:

◆ Gerry and Dunky talking over a pint the night *before* the argument:

Gerry: No, Dunky, I've not got it wrong. I've been going out with Zoe for eight weeks – I know the girl! And I'll tell you this about her . . .

◆ Weeks after the argument, Gerry meets a good friend:

Gerry: No, Zoe finished with me. I blew that one badly. Do you really want to hear about it? Well . . .

Discussion

1 This story features a range of themes: snobbery; false pride; blind prejudice; boy meets girl. You may identify more than this. Take any two of the themes that are linked and show how

the writer presents them to the reader. How do the themes come together?

2   Look at the scenes involving the three funny/weird characters – the Chinese restaurant drunk; the Artist; Dr Nochecky. How do these light-hearted scenes give us a deeper understanding of Zoe and Gerry? Approach this from your knowledge of the 'real' Zoe, and from your view of Gerry's character.

Suggestions for writing
Write a critical response to 'A Picture of Zoe' based on this question:

Although 'A Picture of Zoe' has a boy-meets-girl storyline, it is actually anti-romantic. It is really about a boy discovering the sad truth behind his prejudices. Do you agree?

Sharon, The Ferryman's Daughter

Discussion
◆   Look at the vivid descriptions of Sharon and her boyfriend, John. How do they resemble each other in appearance?
◆   We don't really get to know the boyfriend as a person. What personality features or traits might he share with Sharon?
◆   At first, the other girls treat Sharon with 'studied indifference'; but then she becomes the centre of attention. Why? What is so special about her?
◆   In groups, improvize the girls' discussion at breaktime as they speculate on what has happened to Sharon.
◆   Towards the end of the story we are told that 'A gulf of ignorance is opening' between Sharon and the other girls (p. 59). By referring to the story, explain as fully as possible what this means.
◆   What do you think happens to Sharon at the end? Give reasons for your opinion.

Suggestions for writing
1   Script the conversation that takes place when Sharon is called to the headmistress's office.
2   Write the entries in Sharon's secret diary which she starts to

keep from the day she meets John. Make the last entry the one
she writes on the day she stops coming to school.

3   If Sharon had left school to have a baby, there would probably
have been a Social Work report on her case. Write the *formal*
report that a social worker would write for Sharon's school
file.

The New Boy

Group discussion

◆   Look at the first page of the story. List the different things that
Tam does not like about the new boy. What do you think is
the *real* reason why Tam does not like him?

◆   Tam is intolerant of the way other people – e.g. the new boy –
talk. Does his pal, Alec, agree with him? Quote from the story
to support your answer.

◆   Do you think there is a 'right' dialect and a 'wrong' dialect to
use when speaking to folk? How should you decide which way
to speak?

In pairs

The new boy, Colin, has plenty of patter; Tam's approach to girls
he likes is to punch them on the arm.

Working with another person, script and then act out a
meeting at the bus-stop with someone you fancy. Bumping into
this person might seem to him or her to be accidental, but, of
course, you have planned it all . . . Begin: 'Oh, it's you, – . How are
things?'

Suggestion for writing

This story has a happy ending – mainly because Colin, the new
boy, refuses to respond to Tam's aggressive behaviour.

But there could have been a different, unhappier, ending. Write
that ending by changing two things in the story.

1   Make up a confrontation between Tam and Colin that happens
in the dinner hall. This time, the new boy's response is not
quite so friendly. Find the right place in the story for this event
and write it in.

2 Rewrite the final event of the story, starting after ' . . . Where do you come fae?' (p. 65). Concentrate more on what the boys say to one another than on a fight. Make the ending less happy, but keep it realistic.

The Star

In pairs
◆ This is the story of a strange event that takes place in the life of an ordinary boy. Make a list of all the 'ordinary' details the writer includes. Why do you think he is at pains to stress the boy's ordinariness?
◆ What else can you discover about the character of the boy?
◆ Discuss what *you* do when you feel insulted or neglected.

Group discussion
◆ We can enjoy 'The Star' purely as a fantasy story, but we can also read it for the message the writer is trying to put across. Discuss the different ways in which you could interpret the story.
◆ Do you think dreams have meanings?
◆ Think of all the stories you have read, or films you have seen, in which an ordinary person or an ordinary community experiences a supernatural event. Make a list of these films/stories.

Suggestions for writing – Fantasy Stories
1 Rewrite the ending of the story, starting either from 'he felt insulted or neglected' or from 'What have you there, Cameron?' (p. 68).
2 Make up your own fantasy story in which, one perfectly ordinary Sunday, a boy or girl goes to a fairground, wins something at a stall and then discovers . . .

Barely an Incident

In pairs
'Stereotyping' is an important term in understanding the issues of racial harassment and abuse. It means creating false or simplified

categories or pictures ('stereotypes') of a group of people. Races or nationalities are often stereotyped. For instance, a joke which suggests that all Irish people are stupid is using a racial or national stereotype.

Stereotyping can result in many ridiculous and harmful ideas being associated with groups of people. This story, for instance, contains stereotypical ideas often associated with Chinese people.

In pairs, make a list of stereotypical ideas which are often linked with (a) Scottish people, (b) women.

Group discussion

◆ Research shows that most non-whites in Scotland suffer harassment similar to that suffered by the young couple in the story.

◆ Recall a situation in which you felt harassed or threatened and try to describe it to the group. How did you feel? What did you want to do? Did you react aggressively or did you want to get away? Were you being harassed because you belong to a particular group, e.g. because you are a girl?

◆ What else do you think the boy and girl in the story could have done?

◆ Was it an incident worth reporting to the police?

Suggestion for writing – Describing a Scene

Write a description of an occasion when you were waiting in a lonely, bleak place at night. Record all the visual details, and the sounds. Write about how you felt, and the thoughts that went through your head: wishing the bus would come, anticipating the dangers, thinking somebody looked suspicious, imagining you saw something in the shadows, and so on.

Saturday Song

Discussion

In a group or in pairs, try to dig beneath the surface of this story. Think about the following points:

◆ Why do you think Peter has developed such a problem with the clarinet and the music lessons?

◆ Who gets more from the early stages of the friendship – Peter or Mr Briggs? What is it they both get?
◆ The boy's skin complaint is described several times in the story. Why does the writer do this?
◆ What is it that leads Peter to frighten the old man's budgie to death?
◆ The ending suggests that Peter's mother is unaware of his feelings. What could explain this?

In pairs

Think what it must be like to be old in our modern society. Make a list of all the bad things or problems you can think of. After discussing the list, put a tick beside the points you think something could be done about, and a cross beside the ones you think are just inescapable problems of old age.

Suggestions for writing – Radio Play

Imagine that a neighbour discovers the old man dead, and then informs the police. Suspicions are aroused when it is reported that Peter was seen running out of Mr Briggs's house on the last day he was seen alive. The police go to Peter's house and speak first to his mother. Then Peter, who is upstairs practising his clarinet, is called into the room.

Make up and tape a radio play, starting from the knock at the door. Remember the play will be mostly dialogue. All the action must be conveyed by sound effects, e.g. doors slamming, cups rattling, footsteps.

To be effective, plays need to contain an element of conflict. In your play there could be conflict between the police and Peter's mother, or between the police and Peter. But the strongest conflict is likely to arise between Peter and his mother. Think of some of the unspoken feelings suggested in this story, and how the sudden visit of the police might bring them to the surface.

Staff of Life

Much of this story is written in a local West of Scotland dialect. For example, on p. 84 we find *chuckies*; *poke*; *grooing*; and *hurl*.

List the other Scottish words and phrases you can find. Some of them will be unfamiliar to you, but usually you can work out their meanings by looking closely at the surrounding text.

Discussion
This story is set in a past time when there was as much horse-drawn transport as motorized traffic. Discuss in pairs or groups how the author makes this unfamiliar time seem real to the reader. You could consider:

- how dialogue is used;
- who tells the story;
- the vivid descriptions, e.g. the stable and its workers; Hector, the Clydsedale horse.

Suggestion for writing – Newspaper Article
The tragic accident that kills Hector would have been big news in the local paper of the day. Write a newspaper article that gives an account of the accident and provide it with a suitable headline. Make sure that:

- the style of writing, or *register*, is suited to a newspaper;
- the headline is brief and dramatic;
- sub-headlines are included;
- at least one interview with an eye witness is included;
- actual details are given – name of horse and breed; names of witnesses and of ostlers; where and when accident happened. Invent details that are not given in the story.

Vymura/Fat Girl's Confession/ Almost Miss Scotland

Liz Lochhead's poems are best read aloud or performed. They are often funny, as in the wordplay on famous artists' names in 'Vymura'. However, they also combine humour with serious comment about how women and girls see themselves, and how society sees them, as in 'Fat Girl's Confession' and 'Almost Miss Scotland'.

Role-play
Imagine that the would-be beauty queen in 'Almost Miss Scotland'

decided to 'speak out and convince the other lassies' that the competition was just a cattle show. Role-play what might have happened in the dressing-room. Make sure each character is given a definite point of view before starting.

Debate

Look in detail at how the two girls in 'Fat Girl's Confession' and 'Almost Miss Scotland' see themselves. Do you agree with that view of the female sex? Be prepared to defend your point of view.

Set up a class or group debate on the motion: 'Beauty contests degrade and insult women'.

Suggestion for writing – Letter to a Problem Page

Compose a letter to be sent to a magazine problem page on one of the following topics: Fat and Miserable!; My Friends Think I've No Taste; How Can I Make Myself A 'Real Man'?!

If you can think of another 'problem' that makes people feel insecure or unhappy, then write about that.

The letter can be either funny or serious.

Four of the Belt/Moral Philosophy/ Mr Endrews Speaks

The characters in these poems speak in very different voices. A strict teacher pompously justifies why he is belting a pupil; someone desperately tries to make a friend listen to him/her; a 'posh' headmaster wants to make an impression in his new school.

In groups

Read the poems aloud to each other ('Mr Endrews Speaks' is actually a performance piece of prose). It will take a few readings before you get the voices right, so you may need to help each other.

Group discussion

Four of the Belt

◆ How does Mr Johnstone, the teacher, contradict himself in the first verse?

◆ The idea of 'being a man' is mentioned in each of the first three verses. What, in the teacher's mind, has that got to do with giving or getting the belt?

◆ What do you think is the poet's attitude towards belting? Look in the poem for evidence to support your opinion.

Moral Philosophy

◆ How does the title conflict with the content of the poem?
◆ Look at the shape of the poem on the page. Think about how it sounds. Why has the poet set it out in this way?
◆ How would the poem be different if it were written in Standard English? Would it be better? If not, try to explain why the poem works well in Glasgow dialect.

Mr Endrews Speaks

◆ The piece makes fun of people who talk 'posh'. Can you pick out two examples of this?
◆ What does Mr Andrews think of the pupils in his school? Make a list of the things he says that show his opinion of them.

Suggestion for writing – dialogue

Imagine a scene where a pupil and teacher (who speak in different dialects) have a major confrontation. Script the conversation between them, using any dialects you wish, including your own. The important point is to make the dialogue sound believable.

The Adoption Papers: Chapters 6 and 7

These two excerpts are taken from a longer poem called 'The Adoption Papers', which tells the story of a black girl who has been adopted by a white Scottish couple. Chapters 6 and 7 deal with the girl's childhood years in the 1960s and early 1970s. The story is told through the voices of three people – the daughter, the adoptive mother and the birth mother. In the excerpts given here, the 'voices' are those of the daughter and the adoptive mother, apart from a short section in Chapter 7 ('Olubayo was the colour of peat . . . ', p. 108) which records the words of the birth mother.

Discussion

In groups or pairs, try going through the following discussion points. Many of the questions concern the way people react in difficult situations, and how you think you might react in similar circumstances. So, opinions may differ. Try to allow as many people as possible to express their opinion.

What is the girl's reaction to being told she is adopted? 'Mammy's face is cherries . . . ' This section ends as if the girl is experiencing a dream. For the girl in the poem, what do you think the dream could mean?

◆ Do you think the parents were right to choose a black baby?
◆ If children are adopted, should they be told when they are older? If so, when would be the best time?

Do you think a child who has been adopted loses something? Do you think that, if you were to adopt a child, you would feel it was just as much yours as your own child would be?

◆ Name-calling. Is it something that we should worry about? If you have suffered from it, how have you dealt with the problem? What do you think is the best way to deal with it? How can we stop children calling each other names?

The girl in this poem fights back. Should this be encouraged? Or should she be encouraged to be more passive?

What do you think of the reaction of the mother to the other mothers who come to complain?

Read what is said on pp. 136–7 about 'stereotyping'. How is the girl's teacher guilty of this?

Role-play

Act out the scene where a mother comes to the door to complain about her child being hit and is told by the girl's mother that she will put a stop to the hitting only if the other mother puts a stop to the name-calling. Both mothers are angry.

First, try the scene with no agreement being reached: the complainer refuses to accept that the name-calling is important and the girl's mother refuses to tell her daughter to stop fighting back.

Try the scene again, allowing the mothers to reach some kind of agreement. It won't be easy, because both are angry and continually interrupt each other.

Suggestion for writing – Formal Letter
Write a letter of complaint from the girl's mother or father to the headmaster of the school, after the incident at the dancing lesson. Your letter should explain in a reasonable tone why the teacher's behaviour was wrong, and describe the effects his remarks will have had on your daughter and the other children. Go on to say what you expect the headmaster to do about the incident.

My Grandmother's Houses

Discussion
◆ Make a list of all the things you learn from the poem about the girl's grandmother: her appearance, her habits, the kind of person she is. Some of these points are easy to spot; some require closer study.
◆ What does the poet mean by saying the church women were 'flapping over me like missionaries'?
◆ Does the lady in the big house seem to you to be as pleasant or unpleasant? Why do you think so?
◆ Why do you think the girl sees her grandmother as 'the hunchback of Notre-Dame'?
◆ Why do you think her grandmother is always slapping her and telling her to sit up straight?

Suggestion for writing – Pen Portrait
Try writing a description of one of your own grandparents or an older relative or someone you know well. Include: what they look like, what they wear, what they like to cook and eat, what their house is like, any particular things in the house which fascinate you, things they say, their habits, places they go to or talk about. In fact, include anything, endearing or annoying, which helps to build up a picture of the person you are writing about. Remember, it is all the details, all the things a reader can picture, which help to bring a piece of writing to life.

Eugenesis/Initiation

These two poems by William McIlvanney are very different. The first one takes an ironic and humorous look at an unpleasant science fiction world; the second is a personal account of the death of a father from cancer.

Read the poems in groups and answer the following questions after discussion. The final question on 'Eugenesis' involves a writing task and should be tackled on your own.

Eugenesis

◆ Who are 'they' in the first line?
From the second verse onward, 'They' has a capital 'T'. Why? Events begin on 'the first day' and continue until 'the seventh day'. What events are described in that way in another very famous 'story'?
Look at the following lines and try to say in your own words what the poet means:

The computers had found a formula for plenty (verse 2)
Immortality came wrapped in polythene (verse 4)
Each idea was sterilized before its issue (verse 5)

◆ What do you think the 'four historic letters' are? Why should this word upset the computers so much?
Imagine a short statement is issued to tell people what is happening on each day. Write the seven statements in broadcast style, starting each one: 'Your attention please . . . '

Initiation

Which words in the first verse contrast sharply with the theme of death?
In a similar way, which words in the second and third verses suggest the father's approaching death?
Find out what *initiation* means. Discuss who or what the title of the poem might refer to. Could it have more than one meaning?
Which word in verse 4 sums up the feelings of those who watch the dying man? Give your reasons for picking this word.

◆ How is the punctuation of the last line of the poem different from that used in the remainder of the text? What effect is the poet trying to achieve here?

Not the Burrell Collection/
The Glasgow Subway Poems

'Not the Burrell Collection' can be a difficult poem to understand. However, it contains some very powerful and moving comments on human cruelty. 'The Glasgow Subway Poems' are pure fun and fantasy.

Not the Burrell Collection

◆ Look at the individual 'objects' mentioned in the poem. Can you work out – with your teacher's help – what they refer to?
◆ The poem is actually a long list of things. What do they all have in common?
◆ The poem is about a 'collection', as the title suggests, but why is it called '*Not* the Burrell Collection'?
◆ This type of 14-line poem is called a *sonnet*. Work out its *rhyme scheme*. How does the poet's use of punctuation help to convey the poem's message?
◆ The poet's view of what human beings do to each other is a grim one. Do you share it? Give reasons for *your* view.

The Glasgow Subway Poems

The idea behind these poems is a simple one: ordinary and exotic creatures living and lurking in the city's underground trains and stations. Some of these creatures are pleasant and some are not so pleasant.

Can you invent some more?

Make up two more subway poems, choosing your own creatures. Try to describe their actions in a way that is ordinary . . . but strange.

After the War/Washing the Coins

Read these poems a few times, enjoying the sounds and pictures the poet creates. Then use the following questions to try to tease out some of the poems' meanings.

After the War
◆ What is the main attitude of this group of boys to the recent war, and to the soldiers? Quote some phrases which you think best illustrate the points you make.
◆ Various details in the poem suggest what the boys' play consists of. What is it they do, and how does it resemble the activities of real soldiers?
◆ There is an aspect of war most of the boys have perhaps not fully appreciated. Pick out some of the images or details in the description of their play which suggest this aspect of war.
◆ Why do you think one of the boys runs away?
◆ Which words and phrases suggest what has happened to this boy?
◆ Why do you think the poet has chosen to end his poem by giving us a picture of this boy's life?

Washing the Coins
◆ What physical discomforts does the boy endure while he is picking potatoes?
◆ The poet is one of the local boys. There are also Irish people working as potato pickers. What picture of the Irish howkers can you build up from the poem?
◆ What is meant by the line, 'Among the wretched of the native earth', and why does the poet use it here?
◆ Find the point in the poem where the poet stops referring to himself as 'you', and becomes 'I'. Why does he do this? Think of the differences between his life before and after this point.
◆ The last seven lines of the poem deal with the incident suggested in the title. Why is washing his wages a detail the poet remembers? What do you think the incident represents?
◆ The last line is very difficult to understand. Why does the poet describe the washed coins in this way? Why 'English kings' and 'Britannias'?

The Scottish Song/Oor Hamlet

Listening
These two pieces are the words of songs written by Adam

McNaughtan, the Glasgow folk-singer. To fully appreciate them, you have to hear them being sung. Try to get a hold of the recording or get your teacher to invite Adam McNaughtan to the class, or failing that, ask your teacher to sing one of the songs!

Group discussion

◆ Shakespeare, like other writers who lived in previous centuries, is not read so much in schools as he was at one time. Do you think you should read things like *Macbeth* or Dickens's *Oliver Twist* in your English class, or is it right to put more emphasis on more modern plays and stories? Try to think of both sides of this argument.

◆ Adam McNaughtan's songs usually make use of Glasgow dialect. Try to think of all the advantages his writing gains as a result. Then, think of other types of writing apart from songs and poems. What type of writing could successfully use dialect? Do you think dialect could work well in writing which was not meant to be humorous?

Suggestions for writing – Dialect

1 Think of a famous story with a good storyline, e.g. Snow White and the Seven Dwarfs or Beauty and the Beast. Starting, 'There was this . . . ', write a version of the story in your own dialect. If you feel you can do it, try to write in rhyme.

2 Shakespeare's plays are usually about royalty or the nobility, e.g. Hamlet, the prince who couldn't make up his mind, or Macbeth, the over-ambitious king. Try to write a dialect story which is based on a similar theme, but which is about ordinary people, e.g. 'There was this wumman that wanted tae poisin her husband . . . ' (a humorous story, of course) or, 'There was this man comin hame fae his work when an auld wumman shoutit at him . . . '

3 Take a scene from one of Shakespeare's plays (one where the speeches are not too long) and turn the dialogue into local dialect.